LEO SULLI
PRESENTS

SHE WAS A GOOD GIRL TIL
She Knew Me
2

A NOVEL BY BESTSELLING AUTHOR
KELLZ KIMBERLY

Chapter One

SMOKE

"I don't know what the fuck you muthafuckers heard, but I'm about to tell y'all niggas what the fuck it is. I'm not the type of nigga that's gon have his team running around questioning his moves and decisions. This the last time I'm gon' address and discuss this shit. Speak ya shit or hold ya peace."

I wasn't in the mood to deal with this shit cause I told Juelz to handle it. From what Juelz told me he told these niggas it is what it is, but they weren't trying to hear it. In my eyes, that nigga should've bodied all four of they asses just to show them how serious he was. The only thing that should've been brought to my attention was shit that was already handled. Juelz wasn't use to being in charge, but I was gon' need the nigga to get on board quick and in a fucking hurry.

I couldn't put all the blame on Juelz cause he was dealing with Mitt's old ass and his crew. Mitt was a dude my father put on to handle shit out in Harlem. He and his crew were real loyal to each other and my pops.

It was probably cause all them niggas were old, but they were gon' learn to respect a young niggas mind today.

"Man we just don't understand how working with this new cat is going to help us. I heard bout them Jersey niggas, and they ain't shit nice. We fuck up that's not only your head, but it's ours as well. I'm not trying to go out for anyone else's fuck up," Mitt explained while the other three nodded their head in agreement.

"That's what the fuck you worried about a fuck up?"

"That's not what I'm..."

"That's exactly what the fuck you just said. You worried about someone fucking up and you having to take the fall for that shit. Nigga, don't you understand that being part of The Throne means one for all and all for fucking one? You in this shit; that means you in this shit for life. When you got down, you should've already knew that ya life was at risk. Was that shit not made aware to the three of y'all?"

I glared at all four of them, and they ain't have shit to say. This was the bullshit I was talking about. My father had his squad on some soft shit, and I wasn't here for that, not even a lil' bit.

"Listen, this isn't my father's team no more, it's mine. Any nigga that's trying to be down with The Throne needs to know their life is on the line every time they close their muthafuckin' eyes. The way we move weight you have to do more than look over your fuckin' shoulder. Y'all nigga need to be fuckin' paranoid to the point y'all pull y'all guns out on old fuckin' ladies for looking at you too long. There's no room for pussy ass niggas on my squad, and right now that's exactly what the fuck y'all looking like. So what we gon' do to fix the shit?"

"If you fuckin' with them Jersey niggas, I'm out. They too crazy for my blood," Mitt said, standing up.

"Sit the fuck down!"

"Smoke, I understand you got a role to play for these other two niggas, but you don't run shit when it comes to me. I'm old enough to be ya pops, my G."

"I hear you, Mitt."

I walked from behind my desk, taking my belt off causing my jeans to sag a little. I walked right up on that nigga Mitt. He faced me with his chest poked out, and shit like the niggas old age was supposed to faze me.

"You think this is a role I'm fuckin' playing?" I gritted.

"This shit ain't in ya blood, youngin'. Ya pops was a true thoroughbred. He respected the issues of everyone and tried his best to put their issues to rest. You, my nigga, tryin' to run shit with fear and you ain't gon' get far doing that shit. No real nigga follows a muthafucker they fear. Remember that shit cause you gon' need that shit." Mitt smirked like he just dropped some knowledge and I was bout to switch the fuck up.

"You right I'm not my pops. He's the old school, and I'm leader of the new school. But ayo, since you wanna compare me to my father and shit and tell me I'm playing roles, let's do some role-playing."

"The fuck you.....ARGH!" he yelled out in pain from when I hit his old ass with my belt.

I continued whipping the fuck out of him until he tried to swing on me. I dropped the belt and started going in on his old ass. For every punch he threw, I followed up with two of my own. His crew tried to run up, but my team was ready. Juelz, Bean, and Khy all had they guns out ready to rock a nigga to sleep at my first command. I hit Mitt's ass a couple of more times before yanking his ass up by the collar.

"The only reason I'm letting ya old ass breath is cause my father looks at you like family and if I was to tell him, you tried his only son that family shit would be out the window. I'm not bout to hurt my father cause of some shit you can't rock with. So this is what I'm gon' do, them three niggas you walked up in here with are dead, and they have ya old ass to thank for that. You're gonna walk the fuck out of here and pack up shop. I want you and the rest of ya crew out of my shit in Harlem within the next five hours. When I pop up there, I don't want to see not a fuckin' soul. It better be a ghost town out that bitch, or it's ya life, and I'm just not taking ya life. I'm taking ya whole fuckin' team's life!" I barked.

I stopped talking and the room filled with the sound of bullets flying then the thud of bodies dropping to the floor. I let that nigga Mitt go and turned my back towards him to go and sit back down.

"Nigga, you think you can just talk to muthafuckers, however, the fuck you want and ain't nobody gon' check ya shit!" Mitt spat.

I didn't bother to turn around cause I already knew my boys had shit handled. Mitt was still going off when I took my seat and kicked my feet up on the table.

"You just killed fucking family, and I'm not talking about that fake street family shit you claim to be bout. I mean real fucking family and that shit can't go unanswered." Mitt pulled his piece out ready to light me up I guess. He didn't get the chance cause at the sight of the gun Juelz handled his old ass. Five shots to the chest knocked his ass right the fuck down.

"Damn nigga you ain't have to kill him," Khy told Juelz

"The fuck else was I supposed to do. He disrespected Smoke, and he disrespected me when I told him to let this shit go."

"I hear that shit, but that's Sha's people."

"No disrespect to that nigga Sha, but this ain't his shit no more. He should've taken his people when he left. Chalk the shit up to the game."

"Smoke you ain't gon' say shit bout this?"

"My pops just gon' have to understand. I can't have muthafuckers on payroll, and they don't respect the order of operations." I shrugged. Wasn't much I could say. The nigga tried to kill me, and he got dealt with. He brought that shit on himself. I tried to give him a way out, and he ain't want the shit.

"I get that shit, but you know ya pops ain't gon' rock with this shit."

"Nigga, what you care more bout my fuckin' pops or these muthafuckers respectin' us?" I questioned Khy.

"Both nigga. Ya pops gave this shit to the both of us not just ya ass. You need to start discussing shit before you take action. There could've been a better way to handle this shit. Now we gotta dispose of four bodies and figure out something to tell the team out in Harlem."

"The fuck you want me to do let the nigga blow my head off while I discuss with you what the fuck you want to do? No one got time for that shit. Juelz did what he was supposed to do. For the shit with Harlem, I'll go out and handle that and find a replacement for Mitt's ass."

"Yeah ight, nigga. Just make sure you don't hire some random person without letting me know."

"Anything else you gotta say, ma?"

"Yeah clean this shit the fuck up. I'm out!" Khy spat.

He walked out not dapping anyone up. I ain't know what his problem was, but he was gon' have to fall in line like the rest of these niggas. My pops gave The Throne to the both of us, but that nigga wasn't on the same page with me. I was trying to make money moves and didn't have time to get that nigga in check. So for the meantime I was gon' run shit until he got with the muthafucking program.

"I'll call the crew and have this shit cleaned up. Y'all can get out of here. Make sure everything y'all got on gets burned today! Don't do that shit tomorrow or later on in the week do that shit today and bury the ashes."

"Ight," both Juelz and Bean said.

I dapped them both up and watched them leave out. I grabbed my phone and called the crew telling them to come through. After that, I called Promyse to see what she been up to. I haven't seen her in a couple of days cause she kept asking bout the job I was supposed to hook her up with. I ain't have no real answer for her, so I kept my distance a lil' bit. I was gon' have to face the music soon enough but not before I had something lined up.

"I was starting to think you forgot about me." She pouted answering the phone.

"How could I forget bout someone as beautiful as you? A nigga would be crazy to forget about you, Lil' ma."

"I mean I haven't seen you in a couple of days, and you got me staying in this house all by myself. It's weird being here alone."

"Call Paulie and have her come over."

"Paulie has been caught up in her own relationship the same way I'm trying to be caught up in mine."

"So what you sayin'?"

"I'm saying when your done handling business, come my way. I'll have dinner waiting for you and all."

"The only thing I'm tryin' to eat is between ya legs."

"I can serve that for you too, pa."

I had to hold in my laughter cause Promyse tried her hardest to make that come out seductive. She fell a little short, but it was cool cause my baby was trying.

"I got you, Lil' ma. Give me three hours tops."

"Three hours only, Smoke!"

"You got it," I told her, laughing.

We kicked it on the phone until the cleaning people came through. I hung up and watched the cleanup crew like a hawk making sure they did a perfect job. I knew the risks of being in the streets, but jail wasn't an option for me. I rather die than be locked up the rest of my life.

It took them about two hours to get shit cleaned and back to the way it was. We all walked out together then went our separate ways. I was about to pull off when my phone started ringing. Looking at the screen, I saw it was Lola's hoe ass. I should've just let the shit go to voicemail and blocked her number, but something had me wonderin' what she wanted.

"The fuck you want?" I answered on the third ring.

"I have HIV, and it's more than likely that you have it too," was the words out her mouth. Wasn't no hey daddy when you gon' give me that dick, I miss you or nothing. She hit me with that HIV shit, and a nigga was at a loss for words.

"Smoke! Smoke! Smoke! Talk to me baby!" she cried into the phone.

"You deadass or are you playin' right now?" My voice was even toned, but a nigga was shakin' up. The fuck was I gon' do with HIV? I couldn't live a full life having that shit. I couldn't even live a life with Promyse having that shit.

Fuck Promyse. I thought to myself. This shit didn't just fuck me over; it fucked Lil' ma over too., I told her we were both clean and that she didn't have shit to worry about when I took that V-card. Now here comes Lola with this shit.

"I'm deadass. My doctor told me a little while ago. What are we goin' to do?" she cried.

"The fuck you mean what we gon' do? There is no fuckin' we Lola! You did this fuckin' shit to me!"

"I did this to you? How do I know you ain't give it to me? You were out there fuckin' just like I was fuckin'?"

"Yeah, but a nigga was strapping up every time. This shit's on you!" I barked.

"No, it's not on me cause I make sure to use condoms. Plus, I got tested before you and I slept together, and I haven't slept with anyone since you. My pussy only gets juicy for you daddy," she purred.

"Man, get the fuck off my phone and block this fuckin' number. When I see you, it's one to the head, boom the bitch is dead!" I gritted then hung up the phone.

I threw my shit on the passenger seat then hit the steering wheel a couple of times trying to figure this shit out. There was no way a nigga had HIV. When I fucked Lola, I wore a condom, and that shit ain't break. Shawty was buggin' the fuck out. I ain't have no fuckin' HIV.

Chapter Two

PAULIE

"Khy, I'm just saying I want to see you tonight. My mom won't be back until tomorrow afternoon. You can spend the night with me."

"I'm not tryin' to have ya moms do no pop-up shit and catch me in her crib. She's already not fucking with me."

"Let me worry about my mother, and you worry about putting a smile on my face and keeping me happy."

"I ain't gotta worry bout that shit cause it's a given."

"Does that mean you're coming over?' I asked with a smile on my face hype as hell.

"Yeah man. I'll be there in like an hour. Make sure you up."

"I will be and bring me a frozen lemonade thank you."

"Them shit's nasty as fuck. I don't see how you drink them."

"It's not for you to see just make sure you bring it. I'm trying to dip ya dick in it."

"Oh, word?"

"Word! Now hurry up and get over here."

"Ight."

We hung up the phone, and I fell back clutching my phone. Things with Khy have just been getting better and better. I couldn't get enough of him, and he damn sure couldn't get enough of me. I honestly thought being with Khy would mean I was fighting bitches on the daily. I ain't have to step to one chick yet, and I was cool with that. As soon as bitches started to come out the woodworks, it was gonna be a wrap. I refused to be the girl always fighting over her nigga. I would leave Khy before I ever turn into that type of bitch.

I started scrolling on Facebook to try and kill the time until Khy got here because I didn't want to fall asleep. I saw a couple of status from Lola, and they had me worried. Usually, Lola was posting some cocky shit about how the niggas wanted her and shit. This time her status was a little depressing, and it had me wondering what was wrong. I thought about reaching out, but after the shit she pulled with Promyse, reaching out was out of the question until she apologized. She was in the wrong no matter how you looked at it. I wasn't about to let her think shit was good all because I was worried about her. If shit were really serious, she would give us a call and make shit right.

Thinking about Lola had my mind drifting to Promyse. I closed out of Facebook then called Promyse to see what she was up to.

"Hey Paulie, what's going on?"

"What's wrong with you?" Promyse sounded real depressed, and I wasn't feeling it.

"Nothing—" Before she could even finish telling me that lie I cut her off.

"Don't lie to me Promyse. What's wrong with you? You know I'm here for you."

"Oh really cause lately it's been hard to tell."

"What's that supposed to mean? I text and call you just about every day."

"When was the last time I saw you, Paulie? You act like fucking Khy is the only thing you know how to do now."

"Woah, hold the fuck up. Fucking Khy isn't the only thing I know how to do. It's something I enjoy, and I take every opportunity I can get to fuck him. You can't knock me for that."

"How can't I when you dropped me for some fucking dick?"

"Promyse you chose to move out. I didn't kick you out."

"Of course I chose to move out because that wasn't my home. You haven't even been by my place to see it or nothing."

"Okay. I see where you're coming from, Promyse," I told her, biting the bullet. "I'm sorry I should've been a better friend."

Promyse was right, and no matter how much I argued with her, I couldn't deny that I've been a fucked up friend lately. In my defense, it wasn't my fault. It was Khy's. Khy gave me a rush that I've never felt before. I yearned to be around him to the point I would be with him while he handled some of his daily activities. If I went a day without seeing him, I caught an instant attitude, and the only way for it to be fixed was for him to come around. Call the shit puppy love cause it damn sure wasn't full-grown, but I was feeling him. Regardless of it all, it was no excuse for me to leave my best friend hanging like that.

"You don't have to apologize. I shouldn't have gone off. I've just been feeling so alone lately. My mom's in rehab, you're with Khy, I refuse to say anything to Lola's bitch ass, and Smoke just been acting hella funny lately. All the people I was used to having in my life are just gone."

"What you mean Smoke been acting funny?"

"I haven't seen or heard from him in two weeks."

"Wait you haven't seen or heard from him in two weeks?" I spat through the phone.

"Nope. He was supposed to come over two weeks ago. He told me to give him three hours and he'll be over, but he never showed up. I've been calling and texting him, but both go unanswered. Paulie, I don't even know how to feel about this whole thing. I gave him the best part of me, and then the nigga started acting funny. It makes me believe that sex is all he wanted."

"I doubt sex was all he wanted if he gave your apartment a makeover and sent your mother to one of the best rehabs in the state."

"He could've just done all that shit to hit it. You know money ain't a thing to dudes like Smoke."

"Come on Promyse you can't really believe that cause if you did you wouldn't have laid down with him. You know he's in the streets heavy now since he took over for his pops. That can be the reason why."

My excuse was bullshit, but I didn't need Promyse second-guessing more than she already was. If I were Promyse, I would've done a pop-up visit or fucked some shit up or something just to make that nigga show his face.

"I understand all that trust me, Paulie, I do, but I don't think that's a good enough reason. If he's busy, all he has to do is hit me with a text, and I would back away. He got me ready to ride past his house and shit. Straight Monica style."

"Shut up, Promyse." I laughed hard as hell.

"I'm serious. I just don't understand. It's starting to make me believe all that shit Lola was saying was true. And if it's true then I beat her ass for nothing."

"First, you beat her ass cause she was being disrespectful not because of the shit she said about Smoke. Second, I doubt he's doing anything. If you want I can ask Khy what's been going on with Smoke."

"No, it's cool. I don't want to involve Khy. I just don't get how Khy can find time to spend with you, and I can't even get a callback."

"Khy and Smoke are two different people. You can't compare the two."

"They got different personalities, but they doing the same damn job."

"I get it, but their different personalities are the reason they handle certain situations differently. Khy hasn't let his status get to his head or no shit like that. He's still the same laid back dude he was when he first stepped to me. From what I'm hearing Smoke is letting the shit go to his head."

"Smoke's always been cocky, so that's nothing new. He's just doing what he has to."

"I'm not saying there's anything wrong with how he's acting I'm just pointing out the differences."

"I hear you." She sighed.

"I'm sorry you gotta go through this, but you know I'm down for the pop-up. Matter of fact we gon' spend the whole day together once we wake up. Then when night hits, we gon' pop-up on that nigga. In a cab, cause I don't have time to be taking all them trains and buses to his house and shit."

"I guess."

"What you mean you guess? I call you, and you get on the phone giving me attitude, and then I say we gon' spend tomorrow together and get some answers, and all you can say is I guess? What's really going on Promyse cause it has to be deeper than this shit with Smoke?"

"I don't want to talk about it."

"Don't make me come over there and fuck you up, Promyse. Tell me what's going on."

"My money is running low, Promyse. Like real low. I stopped stripping at the club because Smoke said he would get me a job but he hasn't come through yet. He gave me a few dollars but that's gone, and the money I saved from stripping is just about gone."

"You may not know what to do, but I'm going to tell you what you're not going to do. You're not going back to stripping or working at my uncle's club. What he did was wrong as hell. I don't even understand why he would let you get up there and strip."

"Stripping helped me get good fast money, and that's exactly what I need right now. School will be starting soon, and I need new clothes and supplies. This is my senior year, and I'm not trying to be raggedy like I've been my whole life. Smoke got me some clothes when he did the apartment over, but most of that stuff is for the summer. I don't mind stealing from Rainbow like I used to do, I just don't want to.

Do you know how I felt when I got that makeover? I felt like a whole new person that had confidence on a thousand. I want that feeling back, and I'm not going to get it by wearing clothes from Rainbow or wearing the same clothes from last year. I need money, and the only way to get the type of money I need is to sell drugs or strip. I'm not built for selling drugs, so stripping is my next best option."

"I hear what you're saying, but you can't live above your means when you ain't got them means."

"I'm not trying to live above my means. I'm trying to earn my means."

"I get that but..."

"But nothing. I know you don't approve, but I have to do what I have to do. I can't wait around for Smoke to give me a job. I have to do what I need to do. I don't take my clothes off so realistically I'm just dancing in a bathing suit."

"Yeah okay."

"I don't need you being judgmental; I just need you to support me in this."

"I'm not judging. Hell, I didn't judge Lola for being a hoe, and I'm not going to judge you for being a stripper."

"Thank you."

"No thanks needed you know I got you."

I didn't agree with Promyse stripping, but what could I possibly do? My mother still brought my clothes and gave me money. I didn't have to do anything for myself because it was always done for me. Promyse had to survive on her own and sometimes surviving meant doing things other people didn't agree with.

"Wait, why are you up? It's late as hell, and you know ya ass is usually in bed by eleven."

"I'm waiting for Khy to come over."

"Your mom must be at work."

"You know it." I laughed.

"Paulie, you playing with fire by bringing him in ya moms house."

"I didn't judge you, so I'ma need for you to not judge me."

"This a judgment-free zone I'm just saying."

"Don't say."

"Fine. I'm about to go to sleep. Call me when you're on your way over here."

"Okay."

I hung up the phone trying to figure out what she meant by I was playing with fire. Kids my age snuck their boyfriends into their houses all the time. I wasn't doing anything everyone else wasn't doing. Whenever Khy came over while my mother was at work, I made sure to have Khy out of here an hour before she got home. I had an alarm set, and everything was going to be just fine.

Chapter Three

KHYREE

Chapter Three: Khyree

"Fuck Paulie! That shit cold as fuck!" I spat, pushing her away.

"Just relax I got you." She smiled.

She was in between my legs stirring her frozen lemonade with my dick. I was surprised my dick wasn't soft cause that shit was cold as fuck. She moved the cup then replaced the cold feeling with the warm sensation of her mouth. She slurped the juice off my dick damn near taking my skin with her. The shit felt like a heaven to a god. I gripped the back of her head and started thrusting forward. I expected Paulie to gag, but she held her shit and kept sucking.

"Damn man!" I moaned.

My fingers were all tangled in her hair, and her nails were gripping the shit out of my thigh. I could feel myself ready to bust, but I wasn't trying to bust in her mouth. I let her head go and moved back a little.

"Be still." She told me smacking my thigh.

"Chill out I'm bout to bust," I told her.

"Let the shit go." She looked at me with innocence and seductiveness in her eyes. The mixture was fucking crazy and had my head gone.

Her tongue flicked against the head of my shit. I closed my eyes and enjoyed the feeling. She started sucking hard as fuck on that piece of skin right underneath the head. I was shocked she knew to suck on that shit cause most chicks didn't. Her tongue traveled up and down my shaft and tickled my balls a little. I tried to hold back on bustin' but once she re-dipped my shit in her lemonade and got back to suckin' shit was a wrap. My toes curled a bit, and I let my shit loose. I thought she was gon' move away, but she held shit down like a trooper catching every drop.

"Come give me a kiss." She smirked sticking her tongue out showing me she still had some of my seeds on her tongue.

"Get the fuck out of here with that shit." I mushed not even tryin' to get that freaky.

"You don't want to kiss me?" She pouted.

"Yeah once you brush ya teeth and get that shit out ya mouth."

"Why I gotta brush my teeth? You make me taste my own juices."

"That's different. Ya shit don't swim. I'm not tryin' to

kiss you and feel one of those muthafuckers swimming to the back of my throat and shit."

"You're so stupid." She laughed.

"Call it what you want I'm not with the shits."

"Whatever."

"What time ya mom's get off?"

"Tomorrow afternoon."

"Ight, let's lay down. A nigga gotta get up early to handle something."

I had to go out to Harlem and meet up with this chick I knew from back in the day. With Mitt dead that Harlem spot needed to be filled. Smoke wasn't doin' what needed to be done so I was goin' to handle shit. I didn't know what was goin' on with my nigga, but he's been slippin' lately.

"What do you have to handle?" I looked at Paulie like she was crazy cause she already knew what it was.

"None of ya business. You already know I don't discuss what happens in them streets with you. The two of y'all are separate as fuck, and that's how I plan on keeping it."

"I know but how am I supposed to know if someone is after you if you don't tell me anything?"

"Even if I told you what you gon' do about it?"

"I don't know, but I think I should know. What's the

difference between you telling me what's been going down in the streets and you taking me with you to handle business?"

"The difference is I'm taking you with me but I ain't really doing shit, and ya ass stay in the car. If the cops ever try and question shit, you can't tell them shit cause you don't really know shit to tell."

"Even if I did know, I wouldn't tell them."

"I never said you would, but to keep shit on the safe side, I want to make sure shit stay the way it is."

"Wow!" She spat and stormed out the room.

My ass stayed seated on her bed cause I didn't see the issue. Pillow talking wasn't something I did, and I damn sure wasn't bout to start doing that now. My grandma ain't know about what I was doing out in these streets, so what I look like pulling my girl into that shit. Nah I wasn't with that. The things you love need to remain separate from the street life. That was one of the first lessons Sha taught Smoke and I. I kept that close to my heart and had been living by it ever since.

I grabbed the remote and turned the TV on switching the channel to SportsCenter. I muted the TV, then pulled out my stash so that I could roll a blunt. Paulie would be ight. Her getting upset over dumb shit was becoming the norm. The more she did it, the more I learned to give her the space she needed and shit would be back right. For right now I was cool with it, but the lil' attitude wasn't gon' be a forever type of thing. In the middle of rolling my blunt, my business line started goin' off. People hitting my business line at this time wasn't new. My shit never stopped ringing, which meant money was forever comin' in. I picked my phone up and saw it was Bliss. I answered and hit the speaker button.

"Wassup, Bliss."

"I just wanted to make sure that we're still meeting later today."

"Yeah. I'll text you the address in the a.m."

"It's already the a.m.," she sassed.

"You right, but you know what I mean. Don't play dumb."

"Playing dumb isn't something I do. I'm not on no setup shit, so you can send me the address tonight. If not, then we don't have shit to discuss."

I chuckled cause Bliss' mouth was still something lethal. She ain't play games and didn't give a fuck what came out her mouth.

"I hear you talkin', but we doin' shit my way. If you don't like it, you already know what you can do."

"Come on, Khy baby! You already know how I get down. Hittin' the highway ain't shit for me. The money still gon' come in regardless. Now text me the address, Khy baby..."

"Who the fuck is that on your phone calling you Khy

baby?" Paulie yelled. I ain't even notice her ass was back in the room.

"Ayo, watch ya tone of voice!" I yelled back.

"Nigga, don't tell me what to do like you ain't in my house, in my room, cakin' it on the phone with some bitch!"

"Excuse me but don't ever come out the side of ya mouth callin' me a bitch. Cause a bitch is the last thing you want me to be ight."

"Bitch, you think I give a fuck about you being offended? Get the fuck off my man's line."

"I'll get off his line when I'm good and ready. You better be happy I'm on his line and not on his dick!" Bliss laughed.

"I think you're the one that needs to be happy you ain't on his dick cause I don't play bout this one. A bitch ain't scared to get a murder charge for you thirsty ass bitches." I looked at Paulie as if to say what the fuck. She knew damn well gettin' a murder charge wasn't what she was about.

"Khyree, hang that fuckin' phone up before I grab that hoe through it and beat her ass."

"Sweetie, thirsty is the last word you could EVER use to describe a bitch like me. Let me make this shit clear to you cause I'm not gon' be dealing with this shit. That shit you were just talkin' I'm really about. I don't have a fuckin' problem bringing you that heat if that's what you really want. I don't want Khyree but trust and believe if I did, it would be nothing to have him slidin' in my fat pussy every night."

"Bliss!' I gritted over the bullshit.

"Don't fuckin' Bliss me. Get ya bitch under control. Text me the fuckin' address cause you and that bitch got me fucked up!" Bliss snapped then hung up.

"You really gon' let that bitch talk to me like that, Khyree? Who the fuck is she?" Paulie was all in my face waving her finger and shit.

I lit my blunt and took a pull. Paulie could do all that extra shit on her own. I wasn't saying shit until her lil' ass calmed the fuck down.

"Khy, don't fuckin' ignore me! Who the fuck was that bitch? Why did she feel so fuckin' comfortable callin' you Khy baby? I should fuck you up for being so fuckin' disrespectful. In my house cakin' with another bitch," she continued to yell.

The more she yelled, the more I puffed on my blunt paying her silly ass no mind. After a while, she caught my drift and calmed down. She sat on the bed texting on her phone. I leaned over and snatched the shit out her hands. The only muthafucker she needed to be talking to right now was in the same room as her. I saw it was Promyse and deleted the message she was bout to send.

"What you textin' Promyse for?"

"Wasn't you just ignoring me? The fuck you talkin' to me now for? Just give me back my fuckin' phone.

"Paulie, don't fuckin' play with me."

"You don't want to talk about the bitch, so I'm goin' to talk to someone about the hoe."

"What happens between the two of us stays between the two of us."

"Oh really cause from the way that bitch was talkin' there is no us. She can have you slidin' up in that fat pussy every night."

"Get out my face with that bullshit." I waved her off and went back to smoking my blunt.

"How you just gon' wave me off like ya ass wasn't in the wrong? Then you don't even check the bitch for threatening me."

"Paulie, you threatened her first." I laughed.

"I don't give a fuck; she shouldn't have called you Khy baby."

I put my blunt out and turned to face Paulie. Her anger was written all over her face. Her eyes were squinted low, with her nose turned up and lips poked out. Even with the screw face, she was fine as fuck. I reached out and pulled her closer to me. She tried to fight me off, but her ass wasn't trying hard enough. I laid my body on top of hers and started kissing on her neck.

"Khy stop! We're not having sex after the fuck shit you just did."

"I ain't do nothing tho," I mumbled.

"Who was she, Khyree?"

"A potential business partner."

"If it's business why she callin' you Khy baby?"

"I don't know. You see I wasn't feeding into that shit, so why are you?"

"Mhmm..."

Moving from her neck, I flipped us over, so she was on top. I gripped her waist and looked her in the eyes. She was truly hurt, and even though I didn't see a reason for her to be upset, I was bout to make shit right.

"Look, if I were up to no good you think I would've had that phone on speaker? I put it on speaker cause a nigga don't got shit to hide. Bliss is just some chick from high school. She did a couple of drops for Smoke and me back in the day but nothing major. She was callin' to get the address for our meeting tomorrow. I need her to take over a spot out in Harlem. That's it, ma. Straight business."

"Uh, huh. If you say so. All I know is that you better not bring her ass around me ever."

"I got you. Now fix ya face."

"Nope, I'm still mad at you."

I leaned up and started tickling the shit out of her. She busted out laughing and giggling.

"Stop, Khy stop!" she shouted in between laughs.

"Fix ya face, and I'll stop."

"Ok. Ok." She fixed her face, and I stopped tickling her. She laid on my chest and let out a deep sigh.

"What's wrong, ma?"

"I'm falling for you, and I don't know if that's a good thing or a bad thing."

"It is what you make it. Sit up for a second," I told her.

I reached into my pocket and pulled out a set of keys. I passed them to her then pulled her back down on my chest.

"What's this?" she asked confused.

"I bought me a little spot out the hood."

"Uh okay..."

"Paulie, those are the keys to my spot."

"Are you askin' me to mov..."

"I'm not askin' you to do nothin'. I'm just givin' you keys to my spot. You ain't the only one fallin', ma."

A big ass smile spread across her lips before she kissed me. Our kiss wasn't heavy it was deep as fuck.

Before either one of us knew it, we were naked, and Paulie was ridin' the shit out of my dick. This time sex was different than any other sex we've had. It was filled with emotion and shit. Her moans were more like cries of ecstasy instead of yells. The shit was deep, and I already knew what that shit meant. Ya boy was fallin' in love and shit.

Chapter Four

PROMYSE

Chapter Four: Promyse

"Smoke, I'm not gonna keep blowing up your phone! It's either you call or text me within the next thirty minutes, or we're over. I'm not gonna chase you. I don't know what you're used to, but I'm telling you right now I'm not it."

I listened to the message back and realized how dumb I sounded. His ass pulled a disappearing act on me and here I was still trying to give him more time to get his shit together. I deleted the message and sent his ass a text instead.

Me: It's Over!

I wasn't about to play these types of games with Smoke no matter how much I wanted him. Since he took over, he's become cockier. He acts like the world revolves around him and we're all supposed to kiss his ass. I didn't mind his new behavior because who didn't like a dude with a cocky demeanor. Him going missing on me wasn't something I liked nor was it something I was going to deal with. I had too much on my plate at the moment, and I didn't need him adding to it. My mom was in rehab getting herself together, and I had started back stripping. I went to the club when he didn't show and get my job back that same night Smoke claimed he was coming over.

I was going to tell Paulie that I was back stripping last night. Her response to me thinking about stripping again wasn't what I wanted to hear, so I kept me stripping to myself. Paulie didn't understand my struggle because she never struggled. She liked to believe she knew what I was going through but she didn't. The same went for Smoke. He swore up and down he was going to be here for me, but his ass was nowhere to be found. I didn't have time to hold my breath waiting for the job he was supposed to get me.

To keep myself from going crazy with all the stress I've been feeling lately, I thought about what I was going to do after graduating high school. College was never a thought before because I had to make sure my mother was straight. Dealing with my mother was a fulltime job, and because of that, I slacked in school more than I should've been. I was going into my last year of high school and wanted to make changes and not only in my appearance. I planned on getting my shit together and graduating with the best grades I could get. A four-year college wasn't in the plan, so I had no choice but to settle for a community college.

While I was there, I would get a degree in Liberal Arts just to figure out what I wanted to do with my life. I finally had a chance to put myself first, and I was going to take full advantage of that. I was about to become a whole new person mentally and appearance wise. Before the makeover, I was content with how I looked and the things I had. I wasn't bad looking, but I could've looked a whole lot better. After the makeover, I had this brand new confidence. It showed in the way I looked and the way I moved my body when I was on stage. As bad as some would think stripping was, it really wasn't all that bad. It gave me a chance to work on my self-confidence, and it taught me sex appeal. I was on one and didn't plan on letting anyone throw me off from my goals. I planned on being just as fly as the next chick, and with me stripping again being fly was very possible.

Grabbing my cell phone, I went to my call long to call Paulie and see what she was doing. I needed to talk her out of the pop up she was trying to do on Smoke because I had to work tonight.

"Speak of the devil," I said aloud, looking at Paulie's name flash across my screen.

"I was just about to call you. What Khy got you hemmed up or something?" She was supposed to come over this morning to spend the whole day with me. I figured she would come over, I would cook us breakfast, and then send her on her way back to Khy.

"Promyse, I need you to get over to my house. My mom is buggin' right now!" she panicked.

"Buggin' about what? What happened?" I questioned running to my room.

"Just get over her now! The door will be open. Promyse just hurry!"

"Alright," I hurried up and threw on a pair of shorts and my sneakers.

I hadn't even gotten a chance to brush my teeth or wash my face yet, but Paulie needed me, so all of that was gonna wait. I snatched up my keys, ran out the door, and rushed the short distance to Paulie's house. The elevator was taking too long, so I took the stairs. I climbed them two at a time and by the time I got to her floor I was winded. I took a minute to catch my breath then walked into her apartment.

What the fuck? I whispered to myself when I walked in the house. Clothes, sneakers, jewelry, and anything else that belonged to Paulie was thrown all over the living room. The house looked like a tornado done came through and fucked shit up.

"Promyse, you're here now you can help your disrespectful friend get her shit out my house!" Her mother yelled looking at me. "Did you know she was fucking this boy in my house?"

Her mother was looking at me so intensely that I

froze. I've always looked at Paulie's mom as a second mother. She allowed me to crash here plenty of times when things got to be too much with my mother. Paulie was my best friend, and I couldn't just leave her out here like that, but I didn't want to lie to Paulie's mom either.

"Ma, don't bring Promyse into this. You're doing way too much. It's not that serious. Would you rather me have sex out in the streets or in the house where you know I'm safe?" Paulie asked coming out the room with Khy right behind her.

"I rather you not be having sex at all let alone with this boy. I told you to leave him alone, yet you still mess with him. When did you become so disrespectful?"

"Maybe around the same time you started becoming disrespectful," Khy said.

"Excuse me?"

"Ya excused but ain't no one in ya way. You over here callin' me a boy and shit like I ain't a grown ass man. I get that you don't like me and that shit cool cause I ain't fuckin' with you either, but respect is something that is given. You need to learn to give that shit before you expect it."

"You see the way he talks to me, Paulie? He's going to talk to you the same exact way! I tried to tell you about these no good thugs and how they won't do nothing but leave you hurt, heartbroken, and pregnant. For some reason, you refuse to learn from my mistakes. I refuse to watch you sit here and make the same mistakes I did. You need to pick all this shit up and get the fuck out. You can't stay here no more."

"Ma!" Paulie whined.

"Ma nothing. I told you I didn't want you with this young man, and you disobeyed me. You brought him into my home and had sex with him like you were a grown ass woman. Since you want to act grown, I'm going to show you what the hell grown is. And since you're a grown ass man, I hope you take care of my daughter seeing how she's only seventeen."

"Ya daughter ain't got shit to worry about cause I got her. Believe that."

"Yeah, we'll see. Paulie, I want you out by the time I get back."

I've never seen Paulie's mother as disappointed as she looked right now. She snatched her bag up off the floor and stormed out the door. Paulie fell onto the couch and started crying. I rushed over to her and put my arm around her telling her it was going to be okay.

"Paulie, kill all that cryin' shit. Pack ya stuff and take it over to Promyse's place. I'll be by later to pick you up and bring you home."

"What you mean bring me home? This is my home!" she cried.

"Ya home is with me. Fuck all that shit ya mom was

talking. I got you. I got us," Khy told her, taking her into his arms.

I watched as she cried into his chest, and he let her know everything was going to be alright. It took Paulie a minute to calm down, but once she did, Khy left, and we got to packing her stuff. Nothing was said between the two of us; we just packed in silence. An hour later we were done and had brought everything over to my house. Paulie was laid out on my bed while I was in the kitchen fixing her something to eat. I made her some soup and crackers then brought it to her. She was still laid out on my bed crying softly.

"Paulie, stop the crying cause you know everything is going to be okay."

"How is everything going to be okay? My mom just kicked me out the house and forced me to move in with my boyfriend."

"What did you expect her to do? Why would you let Khyree stay that late at your house anyway?"

"I didn't let him stay late my mom wasn't supposed to be home until the afternoon. Khy woke up to leave out, and we ended up having sex. My mom randomly popped up and caught us. She started going off without even letting me explain myself."

"What was there to explain? She caught you sleeping with the guy she told you to stay away from."

"Promyse, whose side are you on? Cause right now you're sounding just like her."

"You already know I'm on your side, but that doesn't mean I'm not going to tell you when you're wrong. You already knew how ya moms felt about Khy. Why you would sleep with him at your house is beyond me."

"I slept with him at my house because he's my boyfriend. I wasn't going to be out here fucking him in the streets and him paying for hotel rooms was pointless. None of that even matters. What matters is that my mother can't get over what my father did to her. She thinks every street dude is like my father."

"You can't blame her for wanting to protect you."

"Protect me from what, Promyse? Protect me from fucking what? She doesn't even know Khy so how the hell is she going to protect me. She's just mad that my street dude is ten times the man hers was. She's fucking jealous!"

I didn't know what to say, so I said nothing. I doubt Paulie's mom was jealous, but it was clear she was putting her own issues on to Paulie's situation. It wasn't fair, but at least she had a mother who cared.

"Look, I don't want to talk bout this anymore cause it is what it is. I just can't believe I have to move in with Khy. I guess him giving me the keys to his new place is a good thing." Paulie half laughed then dunked her cracker in her soup.

"Wait, he gave you keys to his new place?"

"Yeah, last night." She smiled. "I didn't plan on using them anytime soon, but I don't have much of a choice at this point."

"Well, if you don't want to live with him you can always stay here with me."

"Are you sure?" Paulie asked.

"Yeah. I don't like being here alone anyway. Plus, you've taken me in plenty of times so it's the least that I can do."

"Thank you, Promyse!"

"No need to thank me."

"Yeah well, if you need anything just let me know, and I got you."

"Funny you say that cause I do need one thing."

"I should've seen that coming. Wassup?"

"It's nothing big; I just need you to stay at Khy's house for the night."

"Oh shit, bitch! Let me find out you and Smoke made up," she cheered, smiling big as hell.

"I wouldn't say we made up, but it's something like that," I lied.

"Well, you don't have to tell me twice. Just let me know what time he's coming, and I'll be out of your way."

"Thank you, Paulie." I gave her a quick hug then let her go. "I can't believe we're going to be living together."

"Me either. I can't believe we're going to be living together on our own. You think you and your mom will ever fix things down the line?"

"It's a little too soon to call that seeing how things just happened. I mean it's clear she thinks I'm going to end up just like her. A single mother that does nothing but work and can't get over her first love. I refuse to be bitter like her, and I refuse to let her be right. Maybe when she sees that I'm as smart as she raised me to be, we can work on things, but for right now it's fuck her."

I nodded my head at what Paulie said cause I understood where she was coming from. The worse feeling in the world besides heartbreak is knowing that your mother is no longer in your corner and thinks the worse of you. Paulie was strong, and I was sure she would be able to get through this situation. If there was a time where she couldn't be strong, then I would be that strength for her cause she had been mine for so long. It was crazy how both of our lives had changed in a short period. She was the only constant thing in my life, and I was the only constant thing in hers. It was Paulie and I against the world at this point, but as long as we had each other, we would be straight. I was sure of that.

Chapter Five

SMOKE

Chapter Five: Smoke

Looking at Promyse's text saying shit was over, I laughed. Promyse could think shit was over but wasn't shit over until I said so. I admit I fucked up by ignoring her, but a nigga didn't know what else to do. Lola dropped that bomb on me, and I've been stressed out behind that shit. You know it was serious cause I wasn't even holdin' my weight when it came to the streets. Khy was doing everything on the street front while my ass have been locked up in the crib tryin' to figure out what to do. The logical answer would've been to get tested, but on God, if those results came back positive I was killin' everyone up in that bitch, on some just because shit.

What had me fucked up about the whole situation was how it was gonna fuck with Promyse. She would be dragged into this shit just cause she fucked with me, and she didn't deserve it. Promyse was a good girl who probably didn't need to fuck with a nigga like me. I missed her somethin' crazy. Facing her would just be too hard until I figured this shit out. My time was runnin' out, and I needed to suck it up and get shit in order. Promyse wasn't the only person I've been ducking.

My father has been blowin' my shit down. I was duckin' the fuck out of him cause I ain't feel like hearing his mouth. I already knew he was callin' bout what happened to Mitt. There was no point in even talkin' about the situation. The deed was done, and there was no turning back. If it wasn't for Shai, I wouldn't even been goin' to see him after this meeting I had with Khy. Like I said before there wasn't nothing in this world I wouldn't do for my sister. She wanted to see me, so it was only right I came through.

Slipping my feet into my Nike's, I grabbed my Rolex, car keys, and wallet off the dresser. I headed downstairs just in time to hear this nigga Khy banging on my door.

"I told you to stop banging on my shit like you the police."

"I had to make sure ya ass was still alive in this bitch." Khy laughed, walking through the door.

"I told you to come thru right? Therefore, a nigga good."

"It could've been a setup or some shit. You have been on some other shit lately. You have been a straight ghost, my nigga."

"I've been dealing with some shit," I told him, keeping it short.

"Speak on it then. You know if no one else got you when it comes to shit I got you."

"Ain't nothing to talk about. I got it under control."

"Now ain't the time to be secretive. We're moving into a new business deal and dealing with muthafuckers that got issues with us taking over. We need to make sure we solid on all fronts. Personal and business."

"My personal don't got shit to do with my business."

"You can't say that shit cause your personal had you sittin' out on business for two weeks, my nigga."

"What you couldn't handle it or something?"

"Hold the disrespect cause I don't need that shit. What I'm sayin' is we a fuckin' team, and you need to start actin' like it."

"Yeah ight, nigga. Trust me what I was goin' through didn't have nothing to do with business. I just got hit with some news that I wasn't ready for. I'm good now."

"Good nigga. Just don't let me find out you got a lil' one runnin' around somewhere. We don't need that type of drama."

"Nigga, I strap up every time. Ain't no lil' one of mine runnin' around." I laughed. "Who's this person you got in mind to take over our Harlem spot."

"You remember Bliss, right? The chick that used to do drops for us back when we first started."

"Skinny chick with the nasty attitude?"

"Yeah her. I tracked her down, and shawty's not doing too much. She's in the game, but she's not in the game."

"The fuck that mean?"

"She out here getting money, but she ain't locked into nothing. I figure we give her Harlem and let her hold shit down."

"You sure you can trust her?"

"I wouldn't have set up a meeting if I didn't. She's good money, and her mouth is still slick as fuck. She had Paulie ready to fight her ass through the phone last night."

"What you mean?"

"She called last night tryin' to get the address to the meeting place. I was at Paulie's crib and had the phone on speaker. Out of nowhere shawty starts calling me Khy baby and Paulie wasn't feeling that shit. Paulie told her she would murder her ass, bruh."

"Fuck Paulie know about killin' anyone." I laughed.

"That's what made the shit so funny. She took Paulie straight out of character."

"You already know how Bliss is with her mouth. She

don't give a fuck what comes out of it and dares anyone to speak on the shit."

"She gon' have to calm down with that shit though. Cause Paulie gon' be living with a nigga, and I don't need stress when I go home."

"Nigga, you gon' let her live with you and granny?"

"Nah, she gon' be living with me in my condo."

"Nigga, you got a condo?" I asked shocked. I had been told Khy he needed to move out the hood and get his own spot. He wasn't trying to hear that shit cause he didn't want to leave his grandmother.

"Yeah, nigga. I had to get my own spot. Granny wasn't trying to move and being in the hood wasn't a good look for me anymore."

"Damn nigga, I'm proud of you. How Paulie end up staying with you?"

"I'll explain that shit when we get in the car." He laughed.

On our way to the car, he explained what happened at Paulie's house. The shit sounded like something straight out of a movie. I didn't understand how my boy could get caught slippin' like that.

"How you get caught slippin' like that?" I laughed and pulled off.

"Good pussy will have you fucked up in the head." He shrugged.

"You sure you ready for Paulie to live with you? That shit is a big step."

"What choice do I really have? She ain't got nowhere else to go. The reason she got kicked out is cause of me. I'm not bout to let her be out on the streets. I gave her the keys to the condo before the whole shit with her mom popped off. I ain't think she was gon' be using them this fast, but fuck it. It is what it is."

"I feel you."

We continued talking about business the rest of the way to the meeting. When I pulled up to the spot, I pulled my phone out and sent Promyse a text letting her know I was gon' be swinging through later. Right after that, I sent Shai a text letting her know I would be by the crib tomorrow bright in early. The way Khy stepped up and handled his business when it came to Paulie had me feeling like I had to the do the same when it came to my health. After this meeting, I was gon' head to the clinic and get tested. I wasn't doing that rapid test shit I was gon' do the regular test and just wait for the results. If it came back positive, I would man up and tell Promyse what it was, and then we would go from there. Best believe if the shit came back positive Lola's ass was gettin' a hollow tip with no questions asked.

Chapter Six

BLISS

Chapter Six: Bliss

"You should've beat that bitch's ass. I can't stand an insecure female. All you did was call him baby. You ain't get caught up with his dick down his throat or nothing like that. This why I can't rock with too many females. They too emotional and stupid for me."

"Jiya, shut the hell up cause you sound dumb as hell. You know damn well it's not you that don't rock with females. Females don't rock with your non-likable ass," I joked.

I loved my cousin to death, but she had this way about her that turned any and every one away. I told her time and time again that she needs to go get some help, but she wasn't trying to hear it.

"Fuck you!" She laughed too. "I don't care what you say she would've got this work and then some."

"What did you want me to do? Snatch her through the phone?"

"Hell yeah! Listen, if Soulja Boy can tell a bitch to kiss

him through the phone, then I can tell you to snatch that bitch through the phone."

"I can't stand yo..."

"Bliss, hang up the phone so we can get down to business," Khy said, walking out of the elevator.

"Jiya, let me call you right back," I told her then hung up the phone.

I gave Khy and Smoke the once over and was pleased with what I saw. Both of them were looking like money without wearing anything flashy. It wasn't even what they had on that made them look like money, it was more so their aura that screamed rich niggas. To be honest if I was on some grimy shit, I would've had some of my ladies roll through and stick them up for everything they had.

"It's about time y'all got here. I've been standing in this funky ass hallway for over an hour waiting on the two of you. Y'all don't own phones that tell the time or something?" I snapped slightly.

It was bad enough Khy had me come out to the spot in Harlem that I knew nothing about. Then he had my ass waiting here like niggas wouldn't press me. That's one thing I hated about New York. If niggas saw you in their hood and they didn't recognize you, they would press you to see if ya heart pumps Kool-Aid. They didn't check girls as much as they did the dudes, but nowadays there was no telling what a nigga might do.

"If waiting had you shook then you should go cause shit don't get easier from here," Khy gritted.

"Waiting ain't have me shook. I'm just used to doing business at the time I was told business was going to be handled." I matched his tone of voice because I wasn't about to let him punk me. Nigga or not I was gon' hold my own.

"Kill the back and forth shit cause that's not what we came here for," Smoke said, pushing past us and unlocking the door to the apartment.

I rolled my eyes hard as hell at his back then followed him into the apartment. The apartment was cool to be a trap house, but I was gon' have to switch things up to my liking. I didn't want the place looking like a trap cause that was how you got busted. The house needed to look like someone was actually living here. That way when muthafuckers walked by they didn't think no shady activity was going on.

"Take a seat so we can get shit started." Instead of sitting on the couch, I took a chair from out the kitchen and brought it into the living room.

"Was the couch not good enough for you?" Smoke chuckled.

"It's not. Nine times out of ten the niggas that you had working the spot was fuckin' and getting sucked all over that couch. Knowing how niggas do, ain't no one wipe the shit down. I don't need no dried up sperm or anything else getting on me."

"If it's dried up how's it gonna get on you?"

"I don't know, but I'm not about to take that chance," I told Smoke. "Before y'all tell me how things are going to go let me give you an insight into how I get down." I started to tell them how I liked to work, but Khy started talking before I could get a word out.

"Hol' up I need to make sure we have an understanding about something before we even start talking bout how you like things. That shit you was talkin' last night to my girl was uncalled for. I don't give a fuck what she says to you. You need to show her the utmost respect at all times."

"Oh, that's what you're tripping over?" I asked with a hint of laughter in my voice. I didn't think that bullshit that happened would still have Khy's drawers in a bunch. Yeah, I was pissed last night, but it wasn't deep enough to carry into today's activities.

"A nigga ain't tripping over shit. I'm letting you know what it's going to be. I don't play about a couple of things, and shawty is at the top of the list."

"I'm not tryin' to be disrespectful right now so let me figure out how I can put this nicely."

I paused for a second because I really wanted to be nice about the whole thing. Getting put on with The

Throne was an opportunity of a lifetime. It would solidify me in the game, and that's exactly what I needed right now. I was tired of doing odd jobs here and there for the up and comers. I needed something lucrative and consistent. A bitch had dreams, and I was willing to do just about anything to make them come true. That included biting my tongue instead of giving this nigga a tongue lashing that even his bitch would feel.

"Khy, I understand you wanting to stick up for your girl, but you got me and life fucked up. I'm not about to let your bitch or any other bitch talk to me however she wants. At the end of the day, I'm a woman just like she is. If she wants respect, she's gonna have to give it because if she don't the only thing I got for her is these two fists."

"You got two fists for her, and I got a body bag for you. Come on, Bliss. You heard what the fuck I said. I'm not tryin' to take it there with you, but I will if need be. Show her respect, or you can walk out this door and do business with someone else."

"Khy, you're really gonna give me a hard time for defending myself? That bitch started that shit. All I did was call you Khy baby. It's not like I said I wanted to suck the skin off your dick."

I was trying my hardest to be respectful but the more he talked, the more pissed off I became. He was really trying to check me over a situation that wasn't that deep.

"It boils down to this; you don't make money unless I say so. Anyone that you could go out and work for I got ties to. I can have you in a drought faster than you can call my girl another bitch."

"I can't believe this shit." I sighed, sucking my teeth.

"Believe it cause shit can get ugly. All I'm asking is that you respect my shawty. We don't have to go down that other route. You can either respect her or walk out that door and starve. Either way, a nigga still gonna sleep, fuck, and eat good at night."

"A bitch ain't never gonna starve," I gritted, starting to go in on his ass. Khy had a lot of nerve coming at me about this bullshit.

"Then get the fuck out! We don't need a hard headed nigga or bitch that can't grasp the concept of respect."

"Oh, I can grasp the concept of respect. I just can't grasp this stupid ass concept you're throwing at me."

"It's simple, ma. My shawty is a reflection of me. You don't respect her you don't respect me. Unlike her, I'm willing and ready to kill for my respect. The question is are you ready to take a bullet for your lack of disrespect?"

I looked at Smoke waiting for him to put his two cents into the situation. Khy had a point, but I wasn't feeling the way he was trying to deliver it. What happened between me and his bitch wasn't my fault. No one told her to get all in her feelings cause I called her dude baby.

"Don't look at me cause this ain't got shit to do with me. Y'all need to settle this shit so we can move on. I got places I need to be," Smoke said.

I stood up and thought about leaving. As bad as I wanted to walk out that door, I knew better. I needed this, and I wasn't about to let some bitch fuck it up for me. For the first time in a while, I was gonna bit my tongue. I was gonna respect his bitch, but not because Khy told me. I was doing it because I saw the bigger picture. This was the move I've been waiting for. I would humble myself for the time being. As soon as I found out just who his bitch was, I was gon' beat her ass.

"Ight Khy, you got it. I'll respect ya girl." I had to bit the inside of my cheek to stop myself from telling him to fuck off.

"Good, now let's get down to business," Smoke said, looking at the two of us.

I was glad Smoke stepped in because I wasn't trying to hear nothing else Khy had to say. Back in the day, Khy and I were close so for him to come at me like this hurt a little. Putting my feelings to the side, I listened as they ran everything down to me. For the most part, everything was love. They were giving me free reign to run Harlem how I saw fit which was a plus for me. I didn't need them trying to micromanage the new kid cause I knew what I was doing. All they needed to worry about was me having my money on time. Since I played to have it on time every time, they didn't have shit to worry about.

The only thing I had an issue with was me only getting half of my profits for the first three months. That was straight bullshit in my eyes, because if I was putting in the work, then I needed to be paid for all my efforts and not half. When I questioned them about it, they said it was a part of the probation period. I had a lot more to say about the matter, but I held it in and just went with the flow. I planned on using the next three months to show Khy and Smoke that ya girl wasn't nothing to play with.

"Who gon' be ya second in command? We need to make sure that they check out and everything is everything," Smoke said.

"My cousin Jiya is gonna be rockin' with me. No need to look into her background cause shawty straight."

"That's ya cousin, but you saying that she's straight don't mean shit to us. If she checks out, then we'll be in touch to set something up. If not then you need to have a backup plan," Khy told me.

"I don't need a backup plan cause like I said my cousin is straight. When I'm rockin', lil' mama's rollin'. I wouldn't trust anyone else with my life or to help me with this shit.

"You better hope she checks out."

"Wassup Khy, we got a bigger issue that I don't know about?" Since he stepped off the elevator, his ass was coming at me sideways. First, it was the bullshit with his girlfriend, and now he was giving me hell about my cousin.

"We don't have an issue, Bliss. Everything is cool on my end. I'm sayin' tho when I got down, Sha did a background check on me when Smoke vouched for me something crazy. If Sha didn't trust his own son's judgment, what makes you think I'm bout to trust yours?"

"Nah, you gotta come better than that cause everything you just said sounds like straight bullshit."

"Bliss, this ain't back in the fuckin' day. You're not out here making runs for us, Bliss. You're about to be in charge of a whole fuckin' borough. The stakes are higher and so are the fuckin' risk; not only for you but for Smoke and me too. We can't have anyone on our team that might be a liability or does something to get us caught up. I don't know about this nigga, but I don't plan on going to jail for no fuckin' body."

"She's my blood, I can trust her."

"That's what you're not getting, Bliss. This ain't about who you can fuckin' trust. She's YOUR blood. That bitch ain't got no relation to Smoke or me. Her loyalty doesn't lie with us; it lies with you," Khy said.

"Enough of the bullshit. Bliss, if you got an issue with what we're asking, then this ain't for you, ma."

"Check her out and get back to me when you're ready for the meeting," I told them and stood up ready to leave. "Oh, before I go I got one last thing to say. If we're going to be working together, then I need you to not hold what happened with your girlfriend against me. As long as there's hostility between the two of us nothing's gonna work. I said I would respect her, so you need to let it go."

Neither one of them said anything, so I took that as a sign that I could leave. When I got outside, I jumped on my bike and peeled off. Khy had me fucked up to the point I was ready to fuck some shit up. His bitch better been some bad bitch that looked like Beyoncé or better cause he was acting like she was royalty or some shit.

Other than the stuff with Khy, the meeting went well, and I was happy bout the opportunity that was given to me. I planned on doing some major things cause failing wasn't an option and money was the motive. I already knew Jiya was gonna check out. Jiya was blood, and that meant she was the realest person I could have on my team standing beside me. They could be hesitant all they wanted, but I knew what was up.

The money moves that I was about to make was gon' be on a different level. A bitch was hype and couldn't wait to get to work. That little girl who was told so many times that she wouldn't amount to anything was about to become everything. What I was doing wasn't ideal, but shit it was gon' do more than pay my bills. It was going to give me a chance to reinvent myself. It was going to give me a chance to become the person I was meant to be.

Chapter Seven

PROMYSE

"Hey Smoke is on his way. Do you mind packing a bag and telling Khy to come get you now?" I asked Paulie, coming into the living room.

We spent the whole day sitting around watching movies and eating junk food. It was nice to spend time with Paulie like how we used to, but now I needed to get to the money, and she needed to get gone.

"Why didn't you tell me like an hour ago to start getting ready? You know it takes me at least two hours to get Khy ready." She giggled, getting off the couch.

"He just called me. I didn't know he was going to be coming over here this soon."

"Okay well, let me go pack a bag. I have to text Khy to find out if he can pick me up, but if he can't, I'll just catch a cab to his house."

"Sounds good to me. I'm about to go get in the shower." I left out the living room and rushed to jump in the shower. It was eleven thirty, and I needed to be at the club by one.

James was hesitant about giving me my job back because of Smoke's dumb ass, so I needed to make sure that I was on point. I didn't want to give him any excuse to fire me. I needed this gig like the air I breathed, and I wasn't about to let anyone fuck it up. I plugged my phone up into the portal speaker I kept in my bathroom and scrolled through my phone looking for the song that I've been practicing to for the past couple of days. I needed a new set and a new look along with a new song.

I needed the guys at the club to see what I was working with so they knew what they were missing. My money from the club was good, and now I needed it to be great. Just about everyone in my life let me down. I wasn't about to join the list and let myself down too. When the song came on, I jumped in the shower and started slowly moving to the beat under the water. Practicing dance moves in the shower wasn't the smartest thing to do, but the way the water hit my skin helped me go into a zone that I've never been in before.

"Cause I'm gonna bathe you, play with you, rub you caress you. Tell you how much I've missed you. I just wanna touch you, tease you, lick you, please you, love you, hold you make love to you. And I'm gonna kiss you, suck you, taste you, ride you. Feel you deep inside me ooh. I just wanna kiss you, suck you, taste you, ride you, feel you, make you cum too."

Janet Jackson's sultry voice laid perfectly over the slow raindrop like beat had me feeling myself. I slowly went over my choreography to "Would You Mind" while in the shower and no one couldn't tell me I wasn't killing it. I had limited space so I couldn't go full out, but I was doing the damn thing.

"Promyse, what the fuck are you doing feeling all over yourself and shit?" I heard Paulie yell.

I didn't hear a knock on the bathroom door or anything; I just heard her yelling. When I opened my eyes, she had the craziest look on her face, and she was holding the bag that had my outfit and shoes in it for tonight.

"Paulie, why would you just walking in the bathroom like that? I told you I was getting in the shower."

"Yeah you did, but what you didn't tell me was that you were stripping again!" she snapped.

"What happened to the whole no judgment thing."

"That went out the window the minute you lied to me."

"I didn't lie to you. I just didn't tell you."

"Correct me if I'm wrong, but last night when we talked about it, you were talking like you were thinking about stripping again. Not that you were doing it."

"That's not lying. I wanted to see what you were going to say about the topic. You didn't react the way I wanted you to, so I kept to myself. What's the big deal?"

"The big deal is that Smoke isn't only going to kill James but he's going to kill the both of us too."

"Smoke isn't going to do anything. For one, I'm no longer his concern and don't you think if James really believed that Smoke was going to kill him I doubt he would've let me come back to the club."

"Wait, you're no longer his concern? Promyse, you didn't?" she asked shocked.

I didn't know what she was shocked for. I told her Smoke has been playing me lately. What she thought I was just going to stand by and let him treat me like dirt? I may have been naïve in some areas of life, but I wasn't naïve when it came to how I wanted to be treated.

"Yes I did, Paulie. What else was I supposed to do?"

"Wait, if you broke up with him, is he really coming over here tonight?"

"After I sent him the text saying it was over he hit me back saying he was coming over. I didn't bother replying because I don't plan on being here when he gets here."

"I don't understand. You wanted to see him, and now that he's coming, you're going to play him all so you can go strip?"

"No, I'm playing him so that I can make some money. Stripping is just how I make that money. I'm not going to sit around and allow him to walk all over me. I don't care what business he had to take care of or his street status. I started dating him for who he was, not what he had going on. All I wanted from him was time and attention. I didn't get either one of those things, so I need to move on. If it's like this now between the two of us, I can only imagine how things would be a year or two down the line. He couldn't even keep his promise and get me a job."

"I think you're overreacting a little. I mean I get the whole him ignoring you thing. He needs to pay for that, but the whole job thing I don't think you should hold that against him. He might be doing all that he can to come through for you. Instead of you talking to him about it, you're just going to run back to the same job that he dragged your ass from."

"I'm overreacting yet you wanted to do a pop up on his ass. You don't understand, Paulie. As bad as you want to, I think you need to just chalk it up to the fact you will never understand. I'm not waiting for him to give me anything. I depended on him, he let me down, and now I'm out getting money on my own."

The whole time we were going back and forth I was washing up because I still had somewhere to be. I wasn't going to let Paulie coming into the bathroom stop me from going to work tonight.

"Doing a pop up visit is different from ending things and going back to shaking your ass; it puts people's lives on the line. At least if we did a pop up visit you would know what's real."

"That's the thing at this point I don't care to know what's real. Smoke played me, and I accepted that. As my friend you should respect my feelings even if you don't understand where I'm coming from."

"I can't respect it cause this isn't you, Promyse. Stripping isn't you and doing all this extra shit isn't you."

"Well, this is me. I guess you can say it's the new me. If you don't mind, I need to finish getting ready."

"Promyse, I'm not leaving until we finish this conversation!"

"There isn't anything to finish. I'm done with Smoke. He left me out in the cold with no job, knowing money was my biggest issue. He didn't want me to strip, and I respect that because I thought he would have my back. He couldn't come through for me, and now I'm coming through for myself. What hurts the most about all of this is he knew my struggle and denied my hustle."

"I don't think it's like that," Paulie said, sticking up for Smoke.

I didn't know if there was something she knew that I didn't, but I wasn't feeling the way she was team Smoke. She was my best friend, which meant she was supposed to be on my team and my team only. When I wasn't rocking with Smoke, her ass wasn't supposed to be rocking with him either.

"Then tell me what it's like since you know so much!" I snapped.

"I never said I know so much. Promyse, chill out cause you're getting real snappy."

"I'm not going to chill. You're going real hard for Smoke like you know something I don't. I already lost one friend behind Smoke, so I really don't care about losing the next one behind him." I didn't mean what I said, but Paulie was aggravating me.

"That's how you're feeling? You don't care about losing the only friend you have left?"

"At this point, I don't. I'm tired of everyone being against me. Everyone wants to go against little ole Promyse but when Promyse bosses up everyone wants to play the victim."

"Sweetie, I'm not playing the victim. You're the one coming at me because I'm not bashing your boyfriend. I'm not that type of friend, and you should know that already. I don't jump on a bandwagon because of how my friend is feeling. You already know I'm riding with you to the fullest, but I'm also going to keep it a buck with you. I don't know what's going on with Smoke, but I do think you're overreacting just a little."

"Yeah okay," I told her, getting out of the shower. I grabbed my towel and wrapped it around my body.

"You're really gonna still go to the club?"

"Yeah, Paulie. Just because you feel some way about it doesn't mean I'm going to let that stop me from getting money."

"I understand you're in a bind right now, but this ain't you, Promyse. I'm not going to condone you doing this."

"Really, Paulie?" I couldn't believe she was doing this right now. I need Paulie by my side because at this point I had no one. I needed her to be my support system but all she was being at this moment was a headache.

"You don't have to go, Promyse. You can stay home with me, and I'll help you fill out some job apps. Stripping is the last thing you should be doing."

"Working at a fast food joint isn't going to cut it for me, Paulie. I'm not trying to work just to have enough money in my pocket for food and nothing else. I need money so that I can take care of myself. I don't have a mom around to take care of me. Everything I need to make it in this world, I have to go and get it on my own. I have a whole house that I have to keep up to par with for when she comes home. That takes money, and it takes the type of money I can't get from a regular job. You may not understand because your mom has done everything for you, but this is something have to do. Everyone can't have that perfect life."

"Whose life is perfect because mine isn't. Did you forget that my mom just put me out today? I'm seventeen and moving in with my grown drug dealer boyfriend because my mom doesn't want me under her roof anymore. If that makes my life perfect, then I hate to see what a person's whose life isn't perfect looks like. I'm going through shit just like you. The only difference is I'm not letting it consume me or dictate my next moves. Instead of allowing your issues to take over you, you need to get in front of them and figure out a better way because this ain't it."

"Paulie, I'm not doing this with you right now. I've made up my mind, and if you can't support me during this time, then I don't need your support at all."

I snatched my bag from Paulie then walked around her and left out the bathroom. I went straight to my room and started getting ready. I didn't need this stress right now, and I wasn't going to let it overcome me. Paulie had a damn near perfect life up until recently. This was the first struggle she was going to be going through, and it wasn't even that serious. She had both Khy and me helping her out while no one was helping me out. I had to survive on my own and didn't need her judgment because she didn't like the way I was doing it. At the end of the day, I needed to get it, and I wasn't going to let her stop me from getting it.

$ $ $

Stepping off the stage with my bag full of money, I had the biggest smile on my face. I killed my set, and because I killed it, money was flying all around me. I couldn't wait to get to the back and count up my money to see how much I made. When I got to the back dressing room, it was completely empty, and that was weird because there was always someone back in. I shrugged it off, sat on the floor, and dumped the money out my bag.

"Pretty P, you killed it out there tonight," Mike said, coming into the dressing room. I jointed down the number in my phone so that I wouldn't lose count of my money.

"I'm not trying to be cocky or nothing, but I did a little more than kill it. I murdered that thang, I boasted." Out of everyone in the club, Mike was the only one that I talked to. Mike was the coolest one in the club and always looked out for me making sure I was safe.

"I'm surprised James let you back in here. Ya boy was wildin' the last time you were in here."

"That's not my boy anymore. We broke up," I told him.

"Does that nigga know you not with him anymore?" He laughed.

"Yes, he knows." I paused for second then kept talking. "He even told me he didn't care if I started stripping again. So, you see why I came back. I only stopped because he didn't want me to do it."

"I hear you talkin', but I'm not sure I believe ya story. I don't know much about Smoke, but I do know from the way that he dragged you out of here the first time that he cares for you. And when a street nigga cares for you, he won't ever let you go."

"I'll keep that in mind," I told Mike, rolling my eyes.

"No need to catch an attitude. I just came back here to say you got a visitor."

"Don't let Smoke back here!" I yelled. As much shit as I talked, I knew that if Smoke found out I was in here, he would do more than drag my ass out of here this time.

"Chill out. It's not Smoke, but I'll let this nigga tell you who he is." Mike left out the room before I could tell him that I didn't want to see anyone.

Not even a couple of seconds after Mike walked out, the stranger that I kept running into came walking in taking my breath away. Tonight was the first night that I really looked at him and took in his looks. He was the spitting image of Method Man. Not the Method Man that was doing crazy shit with his hair, but the one that rocked the low cut and was on his grown man shit. He was fine as hell, and the fact that he was a smooth talker didn't make it any better.

"If you don't mind I'm tryin' to count my money," I told him before he could say anything.

"Coutin' money shouldn't even be what you doin'. You're the type to blow money without worrying about how much you spendin'."

"You must have me confused with someone else because blowin' money isn't what I do. I need all the money I can get."

"That's not the only thing you can get." He smirked.

I pulled my phone out and buried my face in it because staring at him was too much. Just from looking into his eyes, I could feel myself drifting away. The feeling he caused me to feel was unreal."

"I'm just sayin' I can be whatever you need and then some. What you thought I was jokin' when I said I could get you off like the weekend?"

"I uh..." I wanted to say something smart but couldn't form the words.

"Give ya man a chance, and we can make magic."

It was funny he brought up magic cause that's exactly the feeling he gave me. It was magical and unreal. It was unlike anything I've felt before, which meant a lot because I hadn't felt many things when it came to the opposite sex.

"Since when did you become my man?" It took all of three minutes for me to form that sentence, but I was happy as hell when I got it out.

"I been ya man, I'm just waiting on you to realize with me is where you need to be. You tryin' to make magic or what?" He walked over to where I sat on the floor and pulled me up. I was happy as hell that he left a little space between the two of us.

"I'm not into the whole fairytale lifestyle so I'ma have to pass."

"Who said anything about a fairytale? I'm trying to give you the real thing. Turn your dreams into your reality on some real shit. I don't fuck with fairytales cause that shit is fake. I only fuck with the real, and the real only fucks with me."

The little space that was left between us became nonexistence when he wrapped his arm around my waist and pulled me close. He cupped my chin and looked deep into my eyes. The smell of his cologne invaded my nostrils and gave me a high I never experienced before. I never cared about how a guy smelled before, but the way this dude was smelling had me wanting to sniff him all day.

"Can you let me go please?"

"Give me a kiss first."

"I'm not kissing you," I told him.

"Why not? My breath doesn't stink, my teeth are pearly white, and I can do some things with my tongue that will drive you crazy. I mean crazy in the sense of keying a nigga's car up and shit."

"None of that matters to me. I don't know your name nor do I know where your lips been."

"I'm trying to put them on you. Shit, I'm tryin' to put them on you every night."

"You don't even know me to be talkin' to me like that. I could be a hoe for all you know."

"Trust me I know more about you than you think. From what I know a hoe is the last thing you are, Promyse Dior White." He hit me with that all American smile. I guess his smile was supposed to put me at ease, but instead, it had me on high alert.

"How do you know my name? Who are you? Are you stalking me? Please don't kill me! You can have all this money just let me live please!" I panicked and started saying whatever came to mind to get me out of this situation.

"Chill the fuck out!" he barked. I shut up real quick and looked towards the ground. "Pick ya head up. I don't care how fuckin' loud I talk, don't ever bow your head to me."

I nodded my head, letting him know I heard him. I didn't know why I was acting like this, but he had me feeling like a child who just got caught doing something wrong.

"Use your words, ma. I don't do that body language shit."

"I heard you."

"Good. I don't need ya money nor do I need to stalk you. I'm good money, and you can believe that. Finish counting your money and meet me outside. I'll be by a white Corvette; you got twenty minutes."

"Where are you trying to take me?"

"Don't question shit I tell you to do. Just do what I say."

"I can't go with you; I have a man!" I blurted out.

"What's that supposed to mean? You got a man not me. As far as I'm concerned that nigga is irrelevant. If he was really ya man, you wouldn't be stripping."

"He doesn't want me..."

"Save the excuse cause I'm not tryin' to hear it. Whatever you and that nigga got going on is y'all business. Tonight, you're my business now finish counting ya bread and meet me at my car."

"Could you at least tell me ya name first."

"Saigon," he replied then let me go.

He kissed me lightly on the cheek then walked out the room. I quickly finished counting my money then took it to the office. James divided our amounts and then I was gone. When I got outside, I saw Saigon to the far right talkin' to someone. I spotted his car and headed in that direction. I didn't know Saigon from a hole in the wall, so there was no way I was getting in his car. When I got to the car I looked towards the direction, I last saw Saigon. He was engrossed in his conversation. I took that as my opportunity to take off because he wasn't paying attention to me. I took off down the street running as fast as I could. I didn't stop running until I came across a gas station. I went inside and asked could I use their phone to call a cab. My phone had died and didn't have any other way to get home.

Twenty minutes later, my cab was pulling up, and I was on my way home. I was beyond tired and couldn't wait to get in my bed and forget about tonight's events. The fight I had with Paulie was weighing heavy on my mind. She was the last person I thought I would get into it with. She usually understood, I just couldn't figure out why she wasn't able to understand this situation. I was going to give a couple of days to get over me stripping then talk to her and try to fix things. Even though I did nothing wrong, I wasn't going to let Paulie fade out of my life like everyone else did.

Chapter Eight
SAIGON

"Yo, what you say to ole girl?" Fame asked laughing.

We were standing outside choppin' it up about nothing too important. I was outside waiting on Promyse to come out. I acted like I wasn't paying her any attention to see if she would listen to what I told her to do. Just like I thought she would, she took off the first chance she got. Shawty was comical as fuck. She probably thought I was gon' kidnap or murder her ass. The only reason I was at the club with Fame was to see if shawty was working tonight. Promyse had been on my mind heavy, and any chance I got to be in her presence, I took it.

"Once she saw you were busy in a conversation, she took off like a bat out of hell. I don't know what you see in her, but you need to leave that alone."

"I ain't say shit to her that she wasn't tryin' to hear," I told him, ignoring the last part of what he said.

"Yeah, ight. You got her all fucked up in the head, and that's not a good look."

"I ain't got her fucked up in the head. That lame ass nigga she fuckin' with got her fucked up in the head. She too busy fuckin' with that nigga when he can't do half the shit I can do for her."

"That same lame nigga is the reason you need to leave shawty alone. We just started doing business with him, and don't need no bad blood."

"You think I give a fuck? Smoke ain't shit but a business partner; what I'm tryin' to do with Promyse is personal."

"What you tryin' to do with her? You don't even know shawty."

"I know enough, and whatever I don't know I'll learn."

"You buggin', my nigga. She ain't shit but a stripper bitc...."

"Fame watch that shit, my nigga. You gettin' real reckless with ya mouth and shit."

"Word, that's what we doing? You gon' check me behind some chick you don't know? Fuck a bitch you don't know, you gon' check me over a bitch that you ain't fuckin' and that got a man?"

"I'm checkin' you cause you talkin' out of term and shit. Don't worry bout what the fuck I got going on. Focus on what you got on your plate my nigga cause what I eat don't make you shit."

Fame was trippin' hard as fuck behind this Promyse shit. I ain't say shit to the nigga when he got our supplier's daughter pregnant. I kept my opinion to myself, and he needed to do the same.

"You got it my nigga, but all I'm saying is you playing with fire."

"I'm not playing with shit. Shawty ain't got a ring on her finger. She not that nigga's wife, but she damn sure is fair game. He ain't doing shit right anyway. She givin' me attention every time I run into her."

"Is she giving you attention willingly or are you backing her into a corner?"

"Say what you need to say, Fame!" I spat.

"I said what needed to be said. Our team don't need no heat, and we don't need no bad blood."

"Since when you start caring bout them niggas? You talkin' bout bad blood and shit, how you think that nigga Khy is gonna feel if he finds out you set him up with ole girl at the club."

"That shit was business, so if the nigga gets mad, that's his business. Come on Sai don't act like I don't know you, nigga. This is what you do. You find a chick that needs fixing and then feel the need to fix her. You did that shit with Emmy, and you're trying to do it with Promyse too. You can't save all these hoes, my nigga."

Hearing Emmy's name sent sharp pains right to a nigga's heart. Emmy was the chick I was gon' give my last name to. She was supposed to be the mother of my child. She was my world, but a nigga wasn't shit to her, but some get back. The crazy thing was ole girl was pregnant with my seed. She killed the baby without a second thought. Fucked up thing was I found the abortion papers the same day I found out she was tryin' to get revenge for some nigga. The shit I went through with her fucked me up for a while. I was just now starting to getting my mind right.

"I 'preciate you trying to look out and shit. I got this handled though. What happens on the personal side of things is exactly that— personal."

"Ight Sai, you got it," Fame said, dapping me up then heading toward the entrance of the club.

Instead of going back in with him, I got in my car and pulled out a pre-rolled blunt from the glove compartment. I took a pull and tried to figure out how I was going to get at shawty. Fame could talk all that shit bout me tryin' to save a hoe cause that wasn't the case. I wasn't trying to save Promyse; I was trying to change Promyse. I wanted to help her reach her full potential. The nigga she's with wasn't gon' do shit but hold her back. I ain't give a fuck what she had going on with Smoke cause her ass ain't give a fuck. She wasn't really bout that nigga cause on more than one occasion she allowed me to get in her personal space. She wasn't foolin' no one. She wanted to fuck with me as much as I wanted to fuck with her. It would only be a matter of time before I got my chance.

Chasin' a female wasn't something I did, but I planned on chasing the shit out of Promyse. Some niggas might've called me thirsty for how I was pursuing Promyse, but those were the same niggas that ain't have shit. A nigga had more money than he could spend, a loving family, more cars than the days of the week, and a big ass house. I had it all. The only thing I was missing was someone to share it with. I was never the type of nigga that didn't give a fuck about these bitches. Since I was youngin' all I wanted was someone to love and someone to love me back. I wanted what my mother and father had, and I wanted it with Promyse.

I knew everything there was to know about Promyse. After my little run-in with shawty at the mall, I had my people look into her. She had a hard life and was still going through the motions. Just from her demeanor, I could tell she didn't deserve the bullshit she was going through. Promyse being as young as she was wouldn't even be someone I took interest in, but it was something about seeing her on that stage that intrigued me. Then it was the little conversation she was offering me that had me wanting to get to know her. Shawty was a good girl who had a hard life. The crazy thing was I could see it in her eyes that she wasn't going to stay a good girl for long. She was fuckin' with a nigga that cared more about clout than anything else. He was too busy tryin' to be that nigga, that he forgot the most important rule about this drug shit.

There should never be one person ahead of the crew because if he dies or goes to jail everyone else in the crew would fall right along with that nigga cause they didn't know no other way besides his. He had Khy as his right hand, but a blind person could see that Smoke was the one calling the shots. Khy wasn't shit but his yes man, if you asked me. I had faith in Smoke cause he came from drug royalty, or should I say hood royalty. Him being Sha's son spoke volumes, but he was still gonna have to prove himself.

Don't get shit twisted I had faith in Smoke when it came to the business, but when it came to the personal side of things, that faith went out the window. Promyse was fair game, and soon enough she would be laying in my bed every night.

Chapter Nine

SMOKE

"Shaheem, when I handed you The Throne I told you that you were gonna have to get a new connect. Right or wrong?" my father asked.

I sucked my teeth at him cause he was asking a question he already knew the answer to. I didn't need this shit right now. I was supposed to be with Promyse fixing shit, but instead of going over there, I came over here. After the meeting, I headed straight to the doctor to get tested. The whole time I was at the doctor's my father was blowing my phone up. I mean he was calling back to back every minute on the minute like he was a bitch that missed the dick.

"Pops, say what you have to say cause these stupid ass questions ain't doing shit but pissing me off."

"I don't give a fuck what's pissing you off. We're going to do this my way and my way only."

"Man, I don't have time for this. Either you get to the point, or I'm out of here, old man."

"You walk out that door, and The Throne is no longer yours."

"Whose else you gon' give it to?" I laughed. "You can't take it back cause you already bowed out. Face it old man; I'm the only one you got to run it."

"Shaheem, the same way I made a way for you is the same way I can take it from you. Did you forget I have a second son? He may not be mine biologically, but he is my son nonetheless."

"You talkin' bout giving the shit to Khy. Ole man you buggin'. Khy don't know what to do with The Throne. If you want your legacy to continue then I'm ya best shot. So wassup you gon' get to the point or am I dippin'."

My father's jaw flinched, and I could see it in his eyes that I was pissing him off. I ain't know what the old man thought this was, but I wasn't having the disrespect. The day he handed everything over to me is the day I became a man. A man in my own right and as a man I wasn't gon' take shit from anyone— father or not.

"The fuck has gotten into you, Shaheem. I handed shit over, and the first thing you do is kill a family friend. Fuck a friend that nigga Mitt was family. You killed his only son and him in the same day. You know how hurt I was to get the phone call from his wife telling me he didn't come home, and if I knew where he was. Then I had to learn that you killed the muthafucker and his son. You're out here wildin' Smoke, and it's not only making you look bad, but making me look bad as well."

"What I do has no reflection on you cause you ain't in this shit no more. The choices I chose to make also don't got nothing to do with you."

"Anything you do is a reflection of me cause you're my son not the other way around. You're right about your choices, they don't have anything to do with me, but they do affect me in ways. Hearing Mitt died cut deep, and you caused that pain Shaheem."

"Look my bad about killin' ya boy. If he wasn't getting out of line and followed orders him and his son would still be alive. What you want me to do pops spare everyone that you look at as family? If that's the case, then I would be sparing the whole fuckin' team. The problem with this whole thing is that you looked at everyone as family instead of looking at them as your workers. Those muthafuckers ain't my blood, and as soon as they fall out of line, my gun will bang, and their bodies will drop."

"Killing isn't the answer to every problem. There is always going to be someone faster than you when it comes to that gunplay. When that time comes you're not gonna have no one looking after you because they gon' be happy that your dumb ass is dead. When you rule with a gun, you end up dying by that shit too."

"What you wishin' death one me?"

"I would never wish death on my own son. What I'm trying to do is tell you what your consequences are going to be for your actions. You can't go around killing anyone that doesn't agree with your way of thinking. I taught you better than that, and it's time that you start using what I taught you."

"I am using everything you taught me just using it in a way that works for me. I 'preciate the talk, but I'm good. My team is good, and my money is even better."

"Ight Sheem, but remember what I said."

"I hear you talkin', old man," I threw over my shoulder as I headed out of his study.

My father was talkin' a whole bunch of bullshit that I wasn't trying to hear. All that shit about ruling by the gun and dying by the gun was straight bullshit. Cause if push came to shove and someone moved faster than me best believe my niggas in the cut would be ready to handle the muthafucker that had the nerve to pull out on me. I wasn't scared about dying cause that came with the territory. The only thing was I didn't have plans on dying anytime soon.

I jumped in my car and was about to pull off when my phone started ringing. It was Paulie's name flashing across the screen.

"Wassup Paulie?" I answered

"You need to get down to my uncle's club and talk some sense into Promyse."

"The fuck is she doing down there?" I questioned.

I told Promyse I didn't want her nowhere near that place. I also told James that if Promyse ended up anywhere near that club that was his life. He must've taken what I said for a joke, but he was gon' learn joking was the last thing I was about.

"She started back stripping because you didn't come through with whatever job you were supposed to get her. She needs the money."

"If she's down at the club where the fuck are you?"

"First of all, watch ya tone when you're talking to me. If I'm being respectful of you, then you need to show the same respect. Second, I tried talking her out of going to the club tonight, but she wasn't trying to hear it. She wanted to be hard-headed, and I wasn't about to chase her."

"So you just let her go the club?"

"What was I supposed to do, handcuff her to the bed or something? Promyse wasn't trying to hear nothing I had to say. I called you because you're the only one that she will listen to."

"You should've done whatever you needed to do to keep her in the fuckin' house. You know the strip club ain't where she need to be."

"Well, if you would've got her a job like you said you were going to, her ass wouldn't be at the strip club. So instead of telling me what I should've done, you need to be worried about what you should've done differently."

"I'll handle it," I told her.

"Yeah, you better or it's ya ass!" she spat then hung up.

I jumped in my whip and pulled off burning rubber trying to get to Promyse as fast as I could. I ain't think her not having a job was going to be a big deal. I told her that I had her, and I meant that shit. She didn't have to work cause I was willing and able to give her whatever she needed. I just needed her to be patient with me. I fucked up by giving her space cause of this HIV shit. Instead of locking myself indoors, I should've got tested and waited for the results. I was buggin' cause it caught me off guard but I should've known better. I just had to wait for the results to be sure, and then I could get shit back on track between the two of us.

In the meantime, I was gon' pull up on her and check her bout the way she was moving. She was out here acting like her nigga didn't tell her not to go back to the fuckin' club. I expected her to listen to what I told her whether I was around her or not. My word was my bond, and I meant what I said to both her and James. Blood was going to shed tonight, and it would be on they hands for disobeying an order.

$ $ $

"Promyse, open this fuckin' door!" I gritted. I was banging and trying to kick her shit in.

It was close to four in the morning, and she had me out here actin' a fool. Before coming over here, I went to the club to see if her hot ass was still there. I tore that bitch up lookin' for Promyse. Her ass was nowhere to be found. Before getting up with James, I called Beans to come through. I needed him to keep James busy until I found Promyse. When he got there, I went through the club for a second time, and that's when I saw Fame coming out the back with the bartender who first told me Promyse was stripping. I dapped Fame up and told him I would get up with him later before snatching up the bartender. I hit her off with a couple of bills, and she started singing like a bird. She told me all about how Promyse was back working in the club and how much money she was pulling in.

When I asked her where Promyse was, she told me that she didn't know. I told Beans to stay at the club until he heard from me then left out headed for Promyse's house. On the way over here, I blew her phone up. She had me out here doing bitch shit all cause she couldn't chill out and wait for a nigga. She didn't answer not one of my calls and after a while her phone started going straight to voicemail. That shit ain't do nothing but piss me off even more.

Promyse was acting out and had no reason to be. She was mad cause I disappeared but that wasn't shit. What was she going to do when a nigga had to go out of town for months? If she couldn't handle what I had going on now she damn sure wasn't gonna be able to handle what I had going on later. She needed to tighten up and tighten up fast. Promyse's innocence is what I admired about her at first.

It was cute and alluring, but that was before I became the king. Now that I held a higher status so did she. The whole good girl thing was no longer a good look. Her innocence was clouding her better judgment, and I couldn't have that. I needed my girl to toughen up and start thinking like the rest of the bitches that came from her hood. A nigga wasn't trying to change her; I just wanted to enhance her. Niggas did it all the time when they gave their girl money to buy fake body parts. I was just gon' do it with her personality and mentality.

"PROMYSE, OPEN THIS FUCKIN' DOOR OR I'M GOING TO KICK THE MUTHAFUCKER IN!" I barked.

I left my key to her crib at home. Carrying it around would've reminded me of my fuck up, and I couldn't have that. Instead, I left everything that reminded me of Promyse in my drawer. The less I had to think about her the better. Now that a nigga done got tested and was just waiting on results, I was ready to get things back on track for when my shit came back negative. I'm not sure why it didn't hit me earlier, but a nigga strapped up when he fucked Lola. There was no way I had HIV, which meant Promyse would forever be mine.

"Smoke, what are you doing here banging on my door like you don't have no sense!" Promyse spat, swinging the door open.

My dick jumped at the sight of her. She was dressed in a sports bra and some small ass bootie shorts. I licked my lips and tried to grab her by the waist. She wasn't having it tho, she pushed me away and folded her arms across her chest.

"Don't touch me, Smoke! We're not together anymore so I don't even know why you're here."

"I'm not goin' anywhere. We need to talk."

"It's a little too late to talk. I don't have anything to say to you. Wherever you been for the last two weeks you can take your ass back. I have enough to worry about without adding you into the equation."

"What you mean adding me into the equation. I never left, ma. Stop playing in let me in. You may not want nothing to do with me but I'm gon' always have something to do with you. I don't just wife anyone or switch up their lifestyle. When I'm invested, I'm invested for life."

"You didn't switch up anyone's lifestyle, Shaheem. You helped me out and I appreciate it, but you can't come inside and we don't need to talk. What we had is over and done with."

"Move out the way so I can come inside." I was trying my best to keep my voice down cause Promyse was trying me. She might've thought what we had was over, but it wasn't over until I was ready to be done with her.

"Smoke, I told you we don't have anything to talk about. Now if you don't mind I would appreciate it if you would... Put me the hell down, Shaheem!" she yelled when I scooped her up in my arms and threw her over my shoulder.

I walked right in the house and kicked the door closed behind me. I carried her over to the couch then threw her down. Looking down at her, I was tempted to rip her clothes off and give her this dick. Fuck giving her the dick I was tempted to put something up in them guts and have her locked down for life.

"Fuck!" I yelled out in frustration. I ran my hand over my face cause wasn't no way I would be able to not fuck Promyse. I should've kept the distance between us until I got my results cause this was gon' be hard as fuck. Since bustin' her open, everything she's does gives off this sex appeal. It wasn't sexy it was more so a nerdy, I ain't never done this before sex appeal. It got me every time and if I didn't switch shit up quick it was gon' have me again.

"Is that all you have to say to me?" she sassed, standing up.

"I heard you started back stripping in the club," I told her.

"Who told you that?" she asked eyes wide.

"Wrong answer, right reaction. I told you I didn't want you stepping foot in that club let alone you dancing in it. Why would you think going back was a good idea?" I questioned.

"I didn't go back. I don't know who told you I did, but they're lying."

If I didn't know the truth I would've believed what was comin' out her mouth. That right there showed me we weren't spending enough time together. I needed to learn her ways, when she was lying or when she was hiding something. I needed to know all of that cause I needed to remain one step ahead of her. Promyse was a diamond that any nigga would be lucky to have. Staying ahead of her would ensure that no other nigga was able to get next to her.

"Promyse, ya lying to me, and I'm not feeling it. Speak the truth or we gon' have a problem."

"I don't even know why Paulie went and told you anything. It's none of her business just like it's none of yours."

"Anything that has to do with you will always be my business."

"I guess that's why you ignored me for the past two weeks. I was your business, but I wasn't your top priority."

"Stop with the bullshit. You're always a top priority but none of that matters. What matters is why the fuck did you go back to the club and start dancing?"

"You're not my father. I can do whatever I want."

"You call me daddy when we fuckin' so a nigga is ya pops."

"Shut up, stupid," she said, laughing a little.

"Ain't shit funny. Why you start back dancin' at the club? You know that nigga's blood is on ya hands, right?"

"His blood isn't on my hands cause I'm not the one to kill him. Did you really kill him?" she asked with worry written on her face.

"It don't matter what I did or didn't do to him. I told you what was gon' happen if he let you back in there."

"You can't blame him. I begged him to give me a job. I need the money."

"When you need money you come to me not no other nigga. That nigga bout to lose his life cause you needed money."

"Stop saying he's losing his life because of me. He's losing his life cause you're fuckin' crazy and need help. How was I supposed to come to you for money when you weren't answering my calls or text messages. I've gotten no fuckin' response from you in the last two weeks, yet you wanted me to come to you for money. How the hell was that supposed to work? I went against my gut and stopped stripping. I depended on you and you did exactly what everyone else did. You let me down. I don't have any more time to depend on anyone. I need to get it on my own and that's exactly what I'm doing. If you don't like it, then that's on you." She was playing it tough, but I saw the tears all in her eyes.

I watched a couple fall from her eyes and my heart started to ache. Letting her down was the last thing I wanted to do. What made it worse was I didn't know she was holding things in the way that she was. I thought she would be mad that I disappeared, but not mad enough to go against my word. I would admit I fucked up but she did too, and two wrongs damn sure didn't make a right.

"I ain't mean to let you down. I just had a lot going on and that needed to be handled first."

"I don't care what you had going on. I was your girl I should've came first or at least second. Hell, I would've settled for coming in third but I couldn't even get that. Khy found time to be underneath Paulie yet you were busy. So that excuse is bullshit in my eyes and you can save it cause I don't want to hear anything else. People make time for the important things in life. It's clear to see what's important to you, and that's your stupid ass empire!" she snapped, slapping me.

I didn't realize she put her hands on me until I felt the sting from her slap. I ain't never have a female disrespect me the way Promyse just did. I blacked for a quick minute and snatched her up then slammed her against the wall.

"Don't ever put your fuckin' hands on me again. I don't hit you so you don't fuckin' hit me," I gritted through clenched teeth. "You comparing me to the next nigga to make a point ain't doing shit but making you look stupid. I ain't like any of these niggas out here. I'm in a league all by myself. If Khy had time to be up underneath his bitch then that's his business. Me and that nigga ain't on the same time, and we don't move the same. We hustle different and because of that, our money is different. If you like how Khy handling business, then go get up with that nigga. I don't have time to be with a bitch fantasizing about the next nigga."

"SHAHEEM LET ME GO! YOU'RE HURTING ME!" Promyse managed to yell.

The pain in her voice brought me back to reality. Once I realized what was going on, I let her go then backed up away from her.

"Promyse I'm..."

"Save it and get the fuck out! How dare you put your fuckin' hands on me because you can't handle the truth! Just get the fuck out!" she yelled again. The tears were coming down a mile a minute at this point. I stood there stuck trying to figure out what to do. I didn't mean to black on her. She just sent a nigga over the edge when she put her hands on me, then talkin' that Khy shit was the last straw.

"Promyse I'm sorry, ma. I ain't mean to put my hands on you." I told her.

"I don't care Smoke. Just get out. Please get the hell out." She sulked. She slid down the wall and fell to the floor.

"Ight ma I'll leave, but know that I'm sorry and it will never happen again. No one has ever been able to piss me off like that. I'm not saying I condone what I did to you, but if you're able to take me there that means you're able to break a nigga too. That shit you said about Khy damn near broke a nigga. I care about you and only want what's best for you."

She didn't say nothing so I started walking towards the front door. Shit was all fucked up, and I ain't have a clue how I was going to get things back on track.

"Don't go," she whispered softly.

"Nah, I don't think I need to be here right now. Things are heated between the two of us and we both need to cool off."

"Shaheem, stay please. I don't want to be alone."

She looked up at me with those watery beautiful eyes and a nigga was stuck. I meant what I said about us needing space to cool off, but how could I leave her when she was like this. I wasn't there for her before, but I could be there for her now. I walked over to where she sat and sat right next to her on the floor. She stretched out and laid her head across my lap. I wiped each tear that slid down her face as we sat in silence.

"Shaheem, I need you. You're the only bright thing in my life, and I don't want to lose you. I can't handle the disappearing. I know you have to work, but I need you by my side too. If it's too much to ask then let me know and I'll try to deal with you missing the best way I know ho..."

"Don't even finish that shit cause you shouldn't have to deal with me disappearing. I'm sorry about that. I'm sorry for the shit that happened here too. I promise I'm going to make it up to you, Promyse. I'm going to fix all this shit and give you the life you deserve."

"I don't need you to give me anything cause I can make a way on my own. I just need you to be there for me. I just need you and your support."

"You got me ma, and you'll always have my support. I know I dropped the ball when it came to getting you a job, but I'm here to make it right now. I'm gon' get you a job on the team."

"What team?" she questioned, sitting up.

"The Throne. If you wanna be with me, then you need to know how I get down and move. Me telling you how shit goes isn't gonna do nothing but make you aware. Being aware is cool but being able to handle shit is better. I know I said I'm in a league of my own, but I'm trying to have you right in that league with me. A nigga can get knocked at any moment, and if I do, I want my girl to be able to handle things. I want you to move the way I move and think the way I think. Ma, you gon' be a female version of me."

I didn't plan on getting knocked no time soon, but I needed to get her to see how serious I was about this. I wanted to keep her close and what better way then to put her on the team.

"I don't think selling drugs is the right job for me. I'm not even that type of girl," She said.

"You ain't the type of girl that strips yet ya ass was doing that. You won't be selling drugs. You will oversee my spot out in Harlem. This is the easiest way for you to make the money that you're trying to see. You know how many bitches would kill to take what I'm offering you."

"Those are probably the same bitches that are used to being a part of the life you live. I'm not like them other girls, Shaheem. I'm not gangster nor am I down enough to oversee anyone's drug operation."

"You gotta have more faith in yourself, ma. How are you saying you can't do something before you fully understand what I'm asking you to do? I don't want you touching shit, no money or drugs. All I need you to do is make sure shit is going the way it's supposed to."

"How am I supposed to get a group of dudes to listen to me? I'm small as hell, and I'm only seventeen."

"That spot isn't run by dudes. We just put a chick in there so you good. I saw the way you got at Lola and that girl Khy was creeping with. If anyone of the chicks get out of line just bring that girl out. You got this. Stop doubting yourself."

"I don't know."

"Think on it then get back to me. I'm gon' be honest with you tho, if you're gonna be messing with me getting down with what I do is gon' happen sooner or later. I'm in this for the long run, and I need to know that my girl is straight and can handle herself."

"You're in this for the long haul?"

"Promyse, I see you as my future. The sooner you realize that and believe it the better off we gonna be. I would never put you in a position that would put you in harm's way. I know it might seem like what I'm offering you will get you hurt, but it won't. I'm offering you a manager's salary without doing all the work a manager does. Just think—"

"I'll do it!" She smiled, cutting me off.

"You don't have to give me an answer right now, just think on it."

"I don't need to think on it. If you believe in me enough to put me on your team when I know nothing about selling drugs, then I need to believe in myself just as much. We're a team, so if you rollin' then I'm ridin' no questions asked, no answers needed."

"That's my bitch!" I boasted, smiling hard as hell.

"Watch your mouth." She hit me in the chest then got off the floor.

"Where you going?"

"To bed, I'm tired as hell."

"Ight, I'm coming with you."

"No, you're not. You're still not forgiven for ignoring me. I may not be hood or street, but I'm not stupid, and I'm damn sure not going to let you walk all over me. You're in time out for the stunt you pulled in here today and your disappearing act. You won't be sliding up in my bed no time soon."

"Damn, it's like that?"

"Yup just like that. We're going to nip it in the bud now, so it doesn't happen again. How you acted today was serious. I'm not going to be dealing with that. If you ask me I'm letting you off easy."

"Yeah okay if anyone is getting off easy it's you. I should bend you over and give you a spanking for going back to the strip club."

"I need money, and I wasn't going to wait on you to get it. I do have one thing to ask you."

"What's that?"

"Don't kill James. I literally begged and cried for my job back. He wasn't trying to give it to me at first. I had to do something I'm ashamed of to get i..."

"Promyse, the fuck you do to get that job?" I asked going from chill to pissed the fuck off in 2.5.

"I...I..."

"Spit that shit out. You never stuttered before don't start now! Did you fuck that nigga?" I barked.

"What?! No, I didn't fuck him. I told him if he didn't give me my job back I would report him for letting me work there and I'm underage."

"You still underage, so why would he go for that?"

"Cause I took it a step further and told him that I would report him to the police too for the advances he made towards me." She hung her head in shame, and I wasn't feeling that shit.

"Pick ya head up cause you ain't do nothing wrong." I was still pissed off but tried to stay calm in the moment. "I see a nigga is starting to rub off on you."

"You're not rubbing off on anyone. I feel horrible for what I did, but I was desperate and really need the job."

"You don't have to explain cause I get it." I let my words trail off cause I started thinking of ways I was going to kill James. At first, he was just going to die because he let my girl strip again. I ain't know the nigga was making advances towards her and shit. Now that I knew, he was going to pay for that shit.

"Just promise me that you won't kill him. I wouldn't be able to live with myself if you did that."

"I can't promise you that."

"Then you might as well get out my house because I'm not dealing with someone who can't refrain from taking a life. You're not God. You don't get to decide who lives and who dies," she sassed. I looked at her to see if she was serious and she was. I ran my hand over my face then pulled her close.

"Ight, you got it. I won't kill him."

"I'm serious, Smoke. If I find out you killed him that's it for us. I won't be with someone who just kills people because they can."

"I wouldn't be killing him just because I can. He disobeyed me and disrespected you. That nigga deserves whatever he got coming."

"I guess it's a good thing he doesn't have anything coming then, huh. I'll see you in the morning. Good night. Make sure you grab some blankets for the couch, playboy." She leaned in and kissed me on the cheek then took off towards her room.

I laughed a little then went to the linen closet to grab a washcloth and a towel. I needed to shower before lying down. Promyse thought sleeping on the couch was a punishment, but I was cool with it. Before stepping into the bathroom, I sent Bean a text telling him to handle the issue. I told Promyse that I wouldn't kill him I ain't shit about anyone else killing that nigga. She could say all that bullshit about being with someone who just killed, but she knew what it was when she started fuckin' with me.

When the hot water hit me, things with Promyse flooded my mind. From me roughing her up to going MIA on her, I was doing shit all wrong. I needed to get us to where we needed to be cause I got plans for the both of us. Promyse ain't know it, but she was about to become my queen to all this shit. Khy was my nigga, but the way we thought was too different for us to rule together. I could mold Promyse to be just like a nigga. Before she knew, she was gonna be a mini-me. I was a king, but I couldn't do that without the strength of my queen. Promyse wasn't there yet, but she soon would be, and when that time came we would be a force to reckon with.

Chapter Ten

LOLA

"Smoke, call me back I don't know why you're hiding from me. We're both going through the same thing, and we need to be there for each other. I know the news I dropped on you was a lot, but I can help you through it. I can help you through a lot. I just need you to call me back!" I hung up the phone after leaving Smoke a voicemail.

I looked at my phone waiting to see if he would call me back. Ten minutes passed, and he still didn't call, so I called him again.

"Smoke, I know you need a release, and I can help you. I can do the things that she can't. I can be that bitch and more. I can be whatever you need me to be. I'll even change the way I dress if that's what you want. I'm trying to be whoever you want me to be, but I can't do that unless you call me back! Please, please, please call me back," I whined. I hung up the phone again hoping and praying that he would listen to my voicemail.

I've been calling Smoke nonstop since I told him I had HIV. Each call went to voicemail, and it was driving me crazy. I didn't understand why he was shutting me out when we should've been dealing with this together. He was the only one I could have sex with, and I was the only one he could have sex with. We needed each other more than ever at this point, but he didn't see it that way. He was going out of his way to not run into me, and I wasn't feeling it.

I would go to all of his hang out spots to try and get a glimpse of him, but he would be nowhere in sight. I took it a step further and would show up to his trap houses, but he was never there. It broke my heart to know that he was ducking me. It wasn't just breaking my heart it was fucking up my physical and mental. With each passing day, my appetite would disappear, and sleep was nonexistent. Nothing seemed to matter unless he was in my life. I didn't even know how he was doing cause Paulie and Promyse still weren't fucking with. I was shut out of his world completely.

Looking at my phone, I thought about calling him back but didn't want to seem too desperate. Instead, I dialed another number. I should've called this person from the jump, but he wasn't my first concern. He really wasn't a concern at all but since I couldn't get in touch with Smoke, calling him would be the next best thing.

"The fuck you doing callin' my phone? I told you after you swallowed my shit that I ain't want shit to do with you."

"Well hello to you too, Khy. I wonder how Paulie would feel to know that I sucked you off while you were getting to know her. I mean you did tell her that you weren't fuckin' with no one. I know her enough to know that she hates liars." I laughed a little.

"I ain't fuck you; I let you suck my dick and gargle my balls. Ain't no lie in my eyes."

"Okay. If you want to look at that way, you're right. But let me ask you this how would she feel if she found out that you're walking around with the package?"

"Lola, get the fuck off my phone with ya bullshit. Ain't nobody got the package," Khy said, sounding so sure of himself.

"That's where you're wrong. I got the package, and if my calculations are right, I could've gotten it from you."

"Bitch, you ain't get that shit from me. Go call whatever other nigga you were fuckin' and tell them that shit."

"I'm just saying you might want to get..."

"Aye Khy, we need to go meet up with Bliss' cousin." Hearing his voice caused my heart to skip a beat.

"Put Smoke on the phone, Khy," I said excitedly.

"I'm not doing shit but hangin' up on ya dumb ass. Word of advice keep ya fuckin' legs closed and stop fuckin' everything with a pulse."

"Hang up on me, and I swear I will tell Paulie that you got HIV!" I yelled before he could hang up.

"Tell her she ain't gon' believe ya ass no way."

"You sure cause I can show her documents that I have it then I'll tell her I sucked your dick to add salt to the wound."

"You an evil bitch you know that," Khy gritted.

"Yeah, whatever just put my man on the phone!"

"Nigga here, it's for you." I heard Khy say.

"Yo."

"Why have you been duckin' my calls, daddy?" I questioned.

I waited for him to say something back, but when the dial tone hit me instead of his smooth voice, I knew he hung up the phone. I let out a high-pitched scream. Something had to give because the more I stayed away from Smoke the worse I felt.

"I'm trying to take a nap. Keep all that yelling down or go outside!" Lala snapped sticking her head in my room.

"I'm frustrated and bored out of my mind. If I want to yell, then that's what I'm going to do."

"Maybe if you make up with your friends you wouldn't be bored. You need to get out the house and clean this room up. It smells horrible."

"I'll clean it when I'm good and ready. Get out!"

"No need to go off on me. Just make sure you clean it today cause I'm having company later."

"Whatever." I rolled my eyes at her and closed the door behind her.

Lala and I were usually close, but now it was like I couldn't stand her ass. I shouldn't have been the one to get the package, Lala or my hoe ass mother should've got it. They were out here fucking way more men then I was, yet I was the one that got hit with it.

"As if my day couldn't get any worse; what the hell does he want?" I spat, looking at my phone.

My doctor was calling me for the third time today. He's been calling me every day, and it was getting annoying. The calls started a week after he gave me my results. I understood that he was just trying to do the job, but I didn't want to hear about my options until I had Smoke by my side. Until Smoke came to his senses, I didn't have nothing to say to my doctor.

I sent my doctor to voicemail then went to my text messages so I could send Smoke a message. If he didn't want to talk to me, then I was going to make him talk to me. The same way I could pull the rug from underneath Khy, I could do the same to Smoke. I knew both of their bitches better than anyone in this world, so it would be nothing to turn their lives upside down.

Me: I think that we need to meet face to face. Before you tell me to fuck off remember that I have a little bit of information that could fuck up your whole world. I'll text you with a place and time when I'm ready to sit down with you. In the meantime just be on the lookout and when you see ME act like you don't know me.

I ended the text with a couple of laughing emojis. Smoke wanted to play, and I was ready to play with his fine ass. While he waited on me to hit him with a time and location, I was going to clean myself and my room up. When I was done with that, I had a couple of people to visit. There was nothing wrong with keeping your friends close and your enemies closer.

$ $ $

"Lola, what was the point in telling us to be here at a certain time if you were just going to show up an hour and a half late?" Paulie snapped.

"I don't know why you're surprised. Lola likes for everyone to be on her time. It always got to be about Lola." Promyse replied.

These bitches ain't gon' gang up on me today. They better simmer down before I turn both of their worlds upside down. It's always about Lola and nothing is going to change that. I thought to myself. I had to bit my bottom lip to keep from saying something smart. I needed them by my side if what I had planned was going to work out.

"I'm sorry I got caught up with my mother, and both of you know how that can be." I let my head hang to make it seem like I was depressed or upset. I needed them to feed into my issues so I could get their sympathy.

"Yeah well, we didn't come here to talk about your mother. Whatever you have to say just say it cause I really don't want to be here."

"Promyse!" Paulie snapped.

"Don't snap at me; it's the truth. I would rather be anywhere but here. Just because she reached out doesn't mean I forgive her for what she did. Her ass didn't even say sorry when she called me."

"Then what did you come here for if you weren't going to hear her out?" Paulie asked her.

I stood back and listened to them go back and forth. Paulie and Promyse arguing was new. They were usually ganging up on me. I guess since I was out the equation they had no choice but to argue with each other.

"Paulie, don't question me about why I showed up because I'm not too sure I want to rock with you either."

"You can be mad all you want, but I did the right thing. You don't see it now, but you'll see it later down the line."

"Whatever." Promyse rolled her eyes then turned to me. "Lola, what did you bring us out here for?"

"Wait what are the two of you arguing about? I didn't even peep how far the two of you are sitting away from each other until now. What did I miss?"

"You didn't miss anything. Now get to the point of us being here."

"That right there is why we're here. I don't know where things went wrong, but somewhere along the line, we started to lose our friendship. I'm not trying to lose the two of you, and I don't want the two of you losing each other. Fighting is something that we do, but we never put hands on each other before. That fight got way out of line and the things I said to you Promyse were wrong. I was just jealous that you had something I wanted. I would say I didn't mean the things that I said, but at the time I did mean those things. I won't take them back, but I will apologize for saying them. A dude should never come between us. We were friends before the dude, and we're going to be friends after him."

"I appreciate your apology, but I'm not sure that we can be friends. The way you acted Lola was out of line. I understand you being upset that me and Smoke are together but I'll never understand why you acted that way. You said a lot of things that hurt and that can't be forgiven."

"Come on, Promyse. She said she was sorry. Getting into arguments over guys is normal. We're young as hell. It's not that big of a deal," Paulie said, sticking up for me.

"It may not be a big deal to you because you weren't the one that was getting hit by those words. Everything Lola said had me feeling like I wasn't worthy of being with Smoke. I wasn't worthy of him because of the things I lacked or what I've been through. We've been friends for a long time, so Lola should've known better than to say that shit."

"I said I'm sorry I don't know what else you want me to say. I'm not gonna kiss ya ass to be my friend. If our friendship meant anything to you, then you would find it in your heart to forgive me. I forgave the both of you for putting hands on me, and I didn't even get an apology. I don't see why you can't forgive me for this."

"She has a point."

"Paulie, since when did you become team Lola? I guess you team everyone but Promyse."

I looked between the two of them trying to figure out what the hell was going on. Something deep had to happen because Promyse was throwing jabs every chance she got.

"Shut the fuck up Promyse because no one is team everyone but you. I don't know what has gotten into you, but I'm not feeling it. You want to be mad at the world when the world didn't do shit to you. Yes, you had a hard life, and that sucks, but I was with you every step of the way. You're mad at me because I told Smoke you were stripping again, but what the hell was I supposed to do. Was I supposed to just stand back and watch you throw away your life because you need fast money? Fast money is cool for the time being, but it's not always good. The things you have to do to get it will haunt you, and I didn't want that for you. You talk about no one being there for you, but when someone is there for you, you want to bitch and complain. Grow the fuck up and get with the program. I'm not one of those friends that's going to tell you what you want to hear. I'm going to hit you with the real raw truth, and I expect you to do the same for me. Whenever I feel like I need to bring Smoke into a situation I will because I know the outcome will be you in a better head space."

I stood there taking in all the drama that I had missed trying to figure out how I could use it to my advantage. Promyse didn't seem to be letting up on Paulie so that I could use her, but Paulie wasn't the one I had issues with. Promyse was the one that needed to reap what she sowed. I didn't care what no one said she stole my man and because of that, she needed to pay. Call me crazy, and I'll be that cause that's what the dick does to a bitch who ain't had that grade A.

"I understand that Paulie, but you didn't have to tell him. Did you know he was going to kill James? You could've got that man killed because you opened your mouth. I appreciate that you're worried about me I really do, at the end of the day tho I'm going to always do what I feel is best. I told you this before you don't understand because you never had to struggle."

"I'm so tired of you saying that bullshit. I understand more than you know, but I'm over this situation. If you want to hold a grudge, then it's on you. I'm not gonna beg for your friendship or beg you to understand where I'm coming from."

"This shouldn't even be going down right now. How the hell did we all fall out with each other?" I sighed. "It shouldn't even be like this. Y'all are my sisters, and I don't see life without the two of you in it."

"I second that last part," Paulie said. We both looked at Promyse waiting for her to say something."

"Ugh! Fine, I guess I love you heffas." She laughed.

"Aw shit, the crew is back together!" I cheered. I went to hug them, but Promyse stepped away.

"We're not back together yet. Lola, you're on a probation period. What you did was fucked up. Yes, I forgive you, but I need time to get over it."

"That's fine with me, and I get it."

"I missed you bitches!" I told them. "My life has been a living hell."

"What's wrong?" Paulie asked.

"Let's go somewhere so we can talk about it."

"We gotta go to Promyse's house cause my mom kicked me out."

"When did this happen?" I asked Paulie.

"I'll catch you up after you tell us about your problems."

On the way to Promyse's house I filled them in on how my mother had come back home and started hoeing out of the house. Everything I was telling them was a lie. Well, the hoeing part wasn't a lie, but her coming back home was. I was laying it on thick to the point both Paulie and Promyse had tears in their eyes. Since they were crying, I had to muster up some tears so I could cry too. I had to the play the role of the depressed friend for a while. It was going to kill me to do it because I wasn't that person, but I was going to make it work. By the time we all graduated high school, Smoke would be mine, and that was on my mama.

Chapter Eleven

KHYREE

"The fuck made you give me the phone when that bitch was on the line?" Smoke asked me once we got in his car.

"She wanted to speak to you, and I made that shit happen." I shrugged.

"Nah ain't no way it was that simple. What the fuck happened?"

"I already told you."

"Nigga, I know you better than anyone else on this earth. You know I'm not fuckin' with her, and for that reason, I know you wouldn't have given me the phone if something didn't happen.

"Ight. A couple of weeks after I started talkin' to Paulie, I let Lola hit me off with some neck. She swallowed my shit, and that was the end of it. Then she hits my line today talkin' about she has HIV and I should go get checked. I told her goofy ass she was buggin' and a nigga was clean. She wasn't tryin' to hear it tho. When she heard your voice, she hit me with the put him on the line or I'ma tell Paulie everything. I couldn't have her tell Paulie shit cause things have been a little rocky with us."

"Damn, she hit you with that shit too?" Smoke said with a hint of laughter.

"What you mean too? Nigga, you knew she had the package and ain't say shit to me?"

"The fuck am I saying something to you for? I ain't know you got down with her, and I wasn't about to let it be known I might be walkin' disease. When she told me that, the shit had me bugged out. A nigga locked himself in the house and wasn't leaving cause of that shit. My head was gone, but I'm good now. I got tested last week and got my test results earlier today. A nigga is clean."

"Congrats my nigga, but you still could've said somethin'. I get you were in a fucked up place, but you ain't' have to deal with that shit alone."

"What were you gon' do have a Dr. Phil moment with me or something? It wasn't for me to talk about. I needed to figure that shit out on my own, and that's what I did. The only thing I regret about how I handled it was leaving Promyse out in the cold. She started back stripping behind that shit."

"Say word?" I said shocked as hell. Promyse wasn't the type to go against someone's word or at least I didn't think she was.

"Word, my nigga. I ran up in that club fast as fuck after Paulie hit my line."

"What James say?"

"That nigga ain't' get a chance to say much of anything. I had Beans handle him. But yo tell me why Fame was up in the club."

"What he out here for?"

"I don't know, but I'm not trusting it. Something bout him seems off. Not off in a bad way, but off in the sense that he doesn't trust us."

"I wouldn't trust us either with the number of bodies you got dropping."

"That shit ain't got nothing to do with him tho."

"But it does. Look at it this way, you get knocked on a murder charge Fame is gon' miss out on money from you. Let's not forget all the product that's out is gonna go to waste, which is another loss since he lets us pay after we sold the work."

"I guess it's a good thing we not getting' knocked no time soon." He laughed.

"Nigga, I don't know why you sayin' we. You're the one droppin' them bodies. I got you on ya books and shit, but I'm not takin' a murder charge for ya ass."

"Damn, it's like that?"

"What you thought it was. I keep telling you to chill out with all that shit but you ain't tryin' to hear. You got it in your head that killin' muthafuckers is gon' make them respect you. That shit makes them fear you and follow you for the time being. Once they see an opportunity, they gon' take that shit and leave you leakin'."

"That's the second time someone spoke on me dying."

"That shit should tell you something. You need to chill the fuck out."

"I am chilling the fuck out. I ain't planning on droppin' no more bodies no time soon. The ones I did drop needed to be dropped cause them muthafuckers couldn't fall in line."

"I hear you. What I'm saying is we can get more accomplished without killing muthafuckers."

"Yeah, ight."

Smoke heard what I was saying, but I knew for a fact the nigga wasn't going to heed to what I was saying. Smoke was my brother ain't no denying that, but the way he was moving was becoming foreign. He got a big ass head out of nowhere and was on some I'm the only nigga in charge shit. I kept how I felt mute cause I didn't want to beef with my brother. As long as the nigga kept it on chill, we would be straight, and the money would come in with no problems.

"I'm thinking bout letting Promyse oversee shit out in Harlem. How you feel bout that?"

"What made you think that shit was a good idea?" Promyse ain't know shit about drugs let alone overseeing a trap house. Putting her in charge would be a dumb ass move.

"She needs a job." He shrugged.

"Then get her ass hired at Taco Bell or buy her a Taco Bell. Putting her in charge of that trap is a bad idea, my nigga. She gon' be a liability. Then we got Bliss up in that spot. You think she gon' be cool with someone as green as Promyse telling her what to do?"

"Bliss will be cool with whatever the fuck I tell her to be cool with. She works for me not the other way around. Promyse needs to learn this street shit ain't no one better to teach her then Bliss. Trust me this gon' work."

"Nigga ain't shit about this gon' work. That shit is a disaster waiting to happen."

"I got this," he assured me.

"That shit don't make this any better. You not thinkin' straight, but I'm not about to waste my breath trying to talk sense into ya ass. You wanna put Promyse up in the trap be my guest. When shit hits the fan make sure you're the one that fixes the issue."

"Ain't I always the one to fix the issue?"

I ain't even respond to that nigga cause he was feeling himself a lil' more than he should be. Before Sha gave us this shit, Smoke and I saw eye to eye when it came to just about everything. I didn't know what the hell changed, but Smoke was acting like everything he said was the right way to do shit.

Wasn't no way in hell letting Promyse oversee Harlem was the way to go, but the nigga wanted to do it, so it was gon' get done. The nigga was blinded by his feelings for Promyse, and it was gon' take shit to fall apart for him to get his sight back. Bliss damn sure wasn't going to listen to anything Promyse had to say. Bliss was the type of chick to shoot a bitch for comin' in between her and her money.

What made shit worse was we were on the way to go meet up with Bliss and her cousin Jiya. If Jiya was anything like Bliss, Promyse was gonna go through hell. I understood Promyse needing money and wanting to work for it, but I don't think overseeing a trap house should be the way to go. Smoke could've got her a job doing anything, yet he wanted her in the streets. I didn't understand that shit. I would never bring Paulie into this shit cause it wasn't even her. On top of it not being her character, I didn't want this for her. She was seventeen and going into her senior year. I wanted her to graduate and go off to college.

Paulie's mom thought I was gon' have her out here looking stupid and shit cause of what I did. I was gon' have Paulie doing the exact opposite. All her dreams were going to come through, and I was gonna make sure she accomplished everything she wanted to. Paulie was gonna be the opposite of me. Just thinking about Paulie put a smile on my face. Shawty was the truth, and I swore I was gonna marry her someday. She just had to get the hang of being in the kitchen. I knew for a fact that her ass knew how to cook but since she's been at my crib, she hasn't touched the kitchen. Her ass didn't even try to clean anything that wasn't her ass. All she wanted to do was lay up in bed and fuck.

Any other nigga would've cool with that, but I wasn't on that. I needed her to move as if she was still living with her mom. I was supposed to talk to her about it this morning, but it slipped my mind when I felt the warmth of her insides. She was the throwing the cat at me every chance she got, and a nigga stayed catching it. I needed things to change cause I couldn't have Paulie falling off. When I got home tonight, I was gon' sit her down and talk to her. I ain't know she told Smoke about Promyse stripping. That was probably why she stayed in the room not wanting to do anything. She was about to get the pep talk of a lifetime, and she ain't even know it.

$ $ $

Walking in the house, I was met by the loud sound of Beyoncé singing at the top of her lungs. I went into the kitchen to see if she cooked something, but it was bare. I headed towards my room to find out what was up with Paulie.

"Why you got the music so loud? I heard that shit before I even got in the door," I told her kicking my sneakers off. She was laid out on the bed in one of my t-shirts and a pair of my boxers. Her hair was piled at the top of her head, and she had her reading glasses on but wasn't reading shit.

"I like to listen to my music loud. It helps to clear my mind. Did you bring the food I asked you to get?"

"Nah, I didn't. Clear your mind for what? Wassup?"

"Why wouldn't you bring the food? What are we supposed to eat?"

"The kitchen is stocked with food, ma. You just have to get up and cook the shit. I've been dicking you down for the last seven days. The least you could do is cook a meal for ya boy," I joked.

"Whatever, Khy!" she spat, rolling her eyes.

"Chill the fuck out I'm only playing with your ass," I told her.

"Yeah right. You were dead serious."

"Matter of fact I was serious. All you been doing is sleeping and fucking. You haven't left out the house or bothered to cook something. All that fast food is gon' catch up with you if you don't watch it."

"I don't give a fuck about it catchin' up to me. What are you saying you're not gonna want to be with me if I get fat?" Attitude laced each word she spit at me. I ran my hand over my head cause this wasn't how the conversation was supposed to go.

"Man, chill with all the attitude shit. I'm just trying to talk to you."

"Then watch what you say, and I won't have an attitude. Talking about all I do is sleep and get fucked. What else am I supposed to do? Up until this afternoon me and my best friend wasn't talking. My mother kicked me out, and I've been in my feelings behind it for the past week. I'm going through something, and instead of you trying to get me to cook ya ass some food you should be here for me telling it's going to be okay."

"I have been telling you it's gonna be okay, Paulie. I'm not about to tell you that shit every hour on the hour. You already know I got you so that bullshit shouldn't be a factor. Ya mom kicked you out it's not that deep. Give it time and things will work themselves out. Just give it time. What happened with you and Promyse?"

"She got mad at me cause I told Smoke about her going to the club. She didn't need to be in that club no way. I don't get why she wants to be there so bad anyway. Ain't nothing in that place but a bunch of hoes."

"You ever think that she knew she didn't need to be there but didn't have any other option but to be there?

"Wait, what?" she sassed, sitting up in bed.

"You heard what I said. Promyse ain't grow up with a supporting mother. She had it hard and working at the club would've made her hard life just a little bit easier.

"So you're saying I should've allowed my best friend to take her clothes off for men and have them degrade her by throwing dirty bills at her?"

"None of that came out my mouth. All I'm saying is telling Smoke may not have helped as much as you think it did. It might've got her into something worse than stripping."

"What could be worse than stripping?"

"I don't know I'm just saying. You should've tried to see things from her point of view and tried to understand where she was coming from."

"Since when did you start sticking up for Promyse and going against me?"

"Paulie, chill the fuck out cause ain't nobody going against you. I'm calling it as I see it, not everything is meant for you to speak on." I wasn't trying to make

Paulie feel bad for what she did, but she did fuck up by going to Smoke.

"Uh, huh. Well okay, the next time you want someone to cook for ya ass call Promyse since you and her are so tight now and you understand her struggle."

"You wildin' the fuck out." I laughed.

Paulie wasn't hearing shit I had to say, her ass was just reacting. As good as Paulie and I were together, we were just as bad. We could never talk about shit without getting into an argument.

"I'm not doing anything. I would think my man would have my back. I did the right thing. I don't care what you say. No matter how hard she has it, she don't need to be stripping in no one's club. As cute as it is that you think you know what's best for Promyse you just met her. I know what's best for her, and what I did was best for her."

"I ain't never say I know what's best for her. All I'm saying is that I understand her struggle."

"Oh and I don't?"

"I'm not saying that."

"Then make it crystal clear what you're saying because you're talking but not saying anything."

"Paulie, you and I both know that you ain't never had it hard in life. Your mother made sure that you had everything you needed and wanted. The worst thing that has happened to you was you growing up in the hood without a father."

"Oh so because we've been dating for all of two months you think you know the worst thing I've been through? Khyree, you don't know shit about me. But let me guess because you've struggled you know what Promyse is going through. Nigga where the fuck did you struggle at? What was your struggle growing up in the hood with your grandmother? That couldn't have been much of a struggle because you're doing a whole lot better than me at this point!" she yelled.

"How the fuck am I doing better than you when I don't have no fuckin' parents? Yeah, ya mom kicked you out, but I'm sure if you went back to her and told her you needed somewhere to say she would let you back in with open arms. I can't fucking run to my mother when shit goes bad. All I got is my grandmother, and yeah I grew up in the hood, but it wasn't with my grandmother.

I grew up in the hood with my alcoholic father who allowed my mother to work and bring home all the money. I grew up with a father who loved to beat my mother every chance he got. The nigga loved to beat her so much that he killed her for coming home ten minutes late. The nigga wasn't real enough to face what he did, so he killed himself. I had to see not only my mother's dead body but my father's too. When it comes to struggling, I know all about that shit cause a nigga been struggling with the death of my mother for years. I've been struggling to forget the images of their two bodies lying on the floor leaking blood. My mother may not have been on drugs, but my father didn't give a fuck about me like her mother didn't give a fuck about her."

"Oh wow!" was all that came out her mouth. I shook my head and got up to grab my sneakers.

"I'm up I'll hit you later," I told her. I left out the room and went straight for the door.

Getting in the car, I didn't have no real destination I just needed to get away and clear my mind. Paulie was taking everything I was saying the wrong way. Instead of listening to what I was really saying, she was just reacting on emotions. I couldn't deal with that shit, and I honestly didn't think I could deal with her. When shit was good between the two of us shit was good. But for some reason, we always found ourselves in these stupid ass arguments.

I didn't have time to be arguing with her over every little thing. She was needed to learn to control her mouth or shit was gon' get ugly between the two of us. All my parents did was argue. I wasn't trying to go through the same thing with Paulie. I was gonna take this one cause I should've minded my business. Promyse being in a trap wasn't my business. She had a mind of her own, and if she was dumb enough to let Smoke talk her into that bullshit, then that was on her. I just needed for Paulie to mind her business when it came to that situation and I would be straight. Wasn't gon' be no monkey see monkey do when it came to that situation.

Chapter Twelve

PAULIE

Sleep didn't come easy after Khy walked out on me. I felt like shit for saying what I said to him. If I would've known his father killed his mother, I would've never let the argument go in that direction. If anyone knew about struggle, it was Khy. His parents' dead bodies were embedded in his head. I could only imagine what he had to do to get over that. Then to deal with the fact your father killed your mother while you were in the other room added on to his struggle.

I didn't try to call him or text him. I let him have his space cause he needed it. The things I said probably brought up all those old memories taking him back to that day. The way I responded didn't help any. I was caught off guard by what he said, so wow was the best thing I could come up with. At seventeen I ain't never heard about something like that happening. I didn't know how to console him at the time, so I said the first thing that came to mind. It wasn't an excuse for me saying something stupid; it was just the truth.

I should've been more comforting to him and told him I was here for him, but I missed that opportunity. The most I could do now was make it up to him. Tonight was gonna be our night. I was going to show Khy just why I was the girl for him. I needed to let him know that I would be there for him through the dark times and the good times. I needed him to know that no matter what I had his back, and he could tell me anything. I haven't been the best girlfriend since we moved in together. Everything he said last night was right; all I did was sleep and have sex. I was too caught up in my own problems to see that I was becoming one of those needy girls.

If Khy wasn't here with me, I was sleeping until he got here, and if I woke up and he still wasn't here, I was calling him to come home. I literally stayed in the bedroom for the past week only eating food that Khy brought for me. Instead of me cooking and cleaning to thank my man for letting me stay with him after only two months of dating, I was sulking in my own misery when I had no one to blame but myself. I fucked up by sexing Khy in my mother's house when I knew that she didn't want him nowhere near her crib. Everything that happened with my mother was on me, and I had to take the blame for it. I wasn't going to sulk anymore I was going to just deal with it. I wanted to be grown, and now I had the chance to be grown. My mother expected me to end up pregnant or heartbroken or both the same way she did. I was going to prove her wrong. I was going to make sure that she saw Khy for who he was. Khy was better than my father was, and my mother couldn't tell me any different.

Tired of thinking about my problems and all the things I've done wrong, I got out of the shower. I dried off, put lotion on, then got dressed all within thirty minutes. I watched the news before getting in the shower. It was supposed to be close to a hundred degrees outside. On days like these, I usually stayed in the house. Since I fucked up last night, I needed to head out and get some things for tonight. The first place I had to go was Promyse's house. I wanted to talk to her about giving Lola another chance. It seemed like we fixed things yesterday, but I knew better. Promyse was keeping her guard up, and a lot of the things she said was very vague. She never went into detail and showed very little emotion towards what Lola was going through with her mother.

I'm not saying Lola didn't deserve that treatment, but if we were going to forgive her, then we needed to do it wholeheartedly and let the past go. Now if Lola got out of line again, then Promyse would have every right to write her off altogether. The only reason I wanted this friendship to work out now was because we all needed each other. It was crazy, but we all just so happened to be on our own. Lola been on her own, and so had Promyse, but with me being on my own I felt we needed each other. Growing up we were all we had, and now it wasn't any different.

Leaving out of Khy's condo, I locked up then jumped in my cab. The ride to Marcy Projects was an hour and a half. I hated that it took so long to get to my girl. When I stepped out the cab, I sent Promyse a text and told her that I would be there in a minute or two. She responded saying the door would be open and to come on in.

"Promyse, where are you at girl?" I yelled, walking in her house.

"I'm in my room give me a second!" she yelled back.

I went to her kitchen to see what she had quick to eat. I saw some waffles in the freezer and pulled them out. I put them on some aluminum foil then stuck them in the oven. I pulled out a plate and the syrup and took a seat at her table.

"I told you to give me a second not to get comfortable," Promyse said, walking the kitchen

"Since when did I have to wait for you to tell me to get comfortable for me to get comfortable?"

"When has there been food in my house for you to get comfortable with?" she joked, but I could tell it hurt her at the same time.

"You've come a long way, Promyse. There's no need to dwell on the past."

"I know. It's just crazy how much my life has changed and how much it's still going to change."

"What you mean still going to change?"

"Nothing. What are you doing here? I figured you would be wrapped up in Khy somewhere."

"He's mad at me. I said something that I shouldn't have, and it pissed him off."

"Paulie, you have to watch what you say sometimes."

"I do watch what I say. I was just upset."

"You never watch what comes out your mouth when you're upset. You gotta work on that, or you're going to lose Khy."

"I know, I know. I plan on fixing things tonight. But, back to you. What's still going to change?"

"I don't even know if I should tell you. I don't need you judging me or anything."

"I'm not going to judge you. I didn't even judge you when you wanted to strip. I just voiced my opinion on the matter."

"Well, if your opinion is anything like it was about the whole stripping thing then keep it to yourself cause I can't deal with any negativity when it comes to this situation."

"No promises. I wouldn't be a real friend if I didn't be honest with you."

"I guess."

"Just spill it."

"Smoke wants me to manage his trap house out in Harlem."

"Come again?"

"You heard what I said, Paulie. Just say what you want to say." She sighed, pulling out a chair.

"I don't have much to say. I mean it's not stripping, but it's not better than stripping either. Promyse, if something happens, you can go to jail."

"I know all of that, but he said I wouldn't be touching money or drugs. I would just be making sure that everything is okay. I don't think I need to go to the trap house. I should be able to meet up with the head worker in charge, and we can discuss everything. I know this isn't the best thing for me to do, but I think it's what I have to do."

"Why in the world would you HAVE to manage a damn trap house?"

I wanted to say more but bit my tongue. I couldn't keep trying to talk Promyse out of situations. As her friend I was gonna have to let her fly or fall on her own. I could only do so much before she realized what was right and wrong for her life.

"Smoke is like the king of the streets, and since I'm with him, I'm kind of like the queen. How am I supposed to be the queen when I don't know anything about this street stuff? I can't even have my man's back because of how naïve and green I am to the things he does."

"So you're saying that you want to become a queen pin?"

"No. I'm saying I just want to have my man's back. He told me yesterday that he sees us together for the long haul. I want that with him, Paulie."

"I'm going to say this, and then I'm not going to speak on it again. Just because you're man does something doesn't mean you need to do the same thing. Having your man's back doesn't really mean that you need to be on some bang bang shoot up type thing. You can have his back in other ways. You're only seventeen, Promyse. You have your whole life ahead of you. You don't want to do something that can possibly ruin your whole life or have you throwing your whole life away."

"Paulie I..."

"Let me finish because I'm not done. Even though I don't agree with what you got going on, I will support you in whatever you decide to do. I'm not saying I'm going to get my hands dirty or stuff drugs in my you know. But, I will be there when you need someone to talk to or when that shit stresses you out."

"I appreciate that Paulie I really do. I don't know if I'm making a mistake, all I know is that I want to be the one Smoke can depend on if things go south. I want to be that chick for him cause I know he would be that dude for me if the roles were reversed."

"Say no more then." I had to end the conversation because if I didn't, I was going to end up telling her just how stupid I felt she was being.

"Thank you Paulie for understanding. It means a lot. Just make sure you don't tell Lola. I don't need her trying some slick shit like getting me put in jail or something."

"You really think Lola will take it that far? Get you put in jail so she can have Smoke. I think that's a little bit of a stretch. She's fucked up, but I don't think she's that fucked up."

"We're talking about Lola here. There is no telling what she would do. If she could talk all that shit about me not being the right one for Smoke, then I don't put anything past her. I'm all for trying to make our friendship work, but it's going to take time for me to trust her again."

"I get it." I shrugged then got my waffles out the oven.

"I'm just saying there is something off about her. I love her cause we grew up together and been through so much, but something is really off about her."

"We all have that crazy side to us. She just shows her crazy side more often than the rest of us."

"She's always showing her crazy side, but that's your friend."

"That's our friend." I laughed.

"I guess, but I have to go. I'm supposed to be meeting Smoke somewhere."

"Damn, I wish you would've told me that before I got here. I wanted you to come to the mall with me."

"You should've called before popping up. I doubt what Smoke has planned is going to take all day. We can go later."

"No, it's fine. I'll bring Lola with me. "

"Let me find out you're replacing me with her."

"You could never be replaced boo; you're my favorite."

"I better be. Here take my key and lock up when you leave. I'll get it from you later."

She took her key off her key ring and passed it to me. I slid it into my pocket then told her I would text her when I was leaving. Since Promyse was gone, I pulled my phone out to keep me busy. I somehow ended up on Khy's message thread. I started to type out a message but deleted it.

"Paulie you're either going to text him or give him space," I said aloud. I threw caution to the wind and sent Khy a text.

Me: I just want you to know that I'm sorry for what I said to you last night. I shouldn't have gotten carried away like that. Khy, I care about you so much and never want to see you hurt the way you were hurting last night. You probably won't respond, and that's fine. I just wanted you to know that I was sorry and I'm thinking of you. I'll see you when you're ready to come back home.

As I hit the send, button tears started to well up in my eyes. I hated and loved the way Khy made me feel. I felt like I was drowning without him but that just showed how much I cared for him. When I hurt him, I ended up hurting myself in the process. At only seventeen, I was experiencing a real-life relationship that came with real-life emotions. I know I said this was puppy love before, but I was lying. There was nothing babyish about what we had; it was full grown.

Chapter Thirteen

PROMYSE

"Smoke, just tell me where we're going. I don't know why it has to be a secret anyway."

"Chill out man. I got you ma. You trust me, right?" he asked me.

"Yeah, I trust you, but I'm not too trusting of being in this car with you while I'm blindfolded. You're not the safest driver."

When I walked out the door, Smoke was outside waiting for me. I didn't even get a chance to get in the car before he handed me the blindfold. I fought him on putting it on, but of course, he won and got me to put it on.

"I ain't gon' kill you so you're good. We're almost there. You'll be able to take it off soon."

"Why are you doing this? Didn't I tell you that I don't like surprises?"

"Nah, you didn't, but I'll keep that in mind for next time. In the meantime, don't look at this as a surprise. Think of it more as an I'm sorry gift."

"What are you apologizing for?"

Even though Smoke messed up and I had him on timeout, him apologizing with a gift wasn't necessary. I didn't need a gift because his actions would be all the gift that I needed. I left all the bullshit that happened between us recently in the past. I was ready to move on and not dwell on it anymore. We had an understanding, and I was good with that.

"The way I've been acting lately. I know shit has been rough, and I never wanted that for the two of us."

"You don't have to go into it cause we talked about it last night. As far as I'm concerned, it's in the past, and that's where I would like to leave it."

"I can respect that, but I'm still gon' say what I need to cause you need to hear it. I can admit I fucked up by leaving you out in the cold, but I swear I only did it cause it was colder inside. I was trying to keep you from the ugly side of things, and because of that, I shut you out. That shit was wrong, and I'm man enough to admit that. You ain't never gotta worry about shit like that happening again. I got you ma. From this point on it's the two of us through all the snowstorms. If you promise to keep me warm, I promise to keep the fire within you burning."

Hearing Smoke talk the way he was lit my soul on fire. His words were simple but intense at the same time. I felt each word in the pit of my soul. I never thought in a million years that at this age I would find someone I wanted to grow with. I didn't just want to grow in life with him; I wanted to grow old with him. Some would say we haven't been dating long enough to have these strong feelings, but when you know someone is right for you no amount of time can change it. I wouldn't say we were in love, but we were on the verge of getting there.

"Don't get mute on me now, Promyse. I'm keeping it a buck with you. I need to know if you hear me cause everything I'm saying is true."

"I hear you I just don't know what to say. What you just said was deep, and I can't start to form something that is as deep as what you said to me."

"This ain't about you showing me what I just showed you. I already know in due time you will let me in on your feelings. For right now, I just want you to know where I'm coming from. I want you to know where I'm coming from so you can see where I'm trying to go with you. I want you to understand that I fucked up, and that shit won't happen again. We gon' move as a unit or we not moving at all."

"Then can we move as a unity and take this blindfold off," I joked.

"You can take it off in ten minutes." He laughed at me.

"Ugh." I sighed.

"Let me find out my baby is turning into a brat."

"I'm not a brat; I just don't want this on my face anymore. Surprises make me nervous and anxious. When I get like that I always have to go number two," I told him.

"You mean number two as in shit?"

"What other number two is there?"

"Lil' ma I'ma need you to hold that in until after the surprise. Matter of fact you need to use the bathroom before the surprise. I don't need you shittin' on yourself from the excitement."

"I'm not going to shit on myself. I got this," I assured him.

"You sure? Cause if you do from here on out your name will be shitty."

"You wouldn't call me that."

"Yes, the fuck I would. I'll call you that all out in public too. So watch that shit." He laughed at his own joke.

"Whatever. Can you just drive a little bit faster so we can get this over with."

"Ease up. Don't get mad."

"I'm not mad; I'm just saying hurry up."

"We here," he said, sounding happy as hell.

The car came to a stop, and I heard his door open then close. I impatiently waited for him to come and get me out the car.

"Hold my hand, so ya ass don't fall. I don't need you getting hurt," he told me once I was out the car.

"If I fall it'll be your fault."

"Yeah, ight."

He held my hand in his and didn't say another word. He helped me walk through wherever we were, and after about five minutes of walking, we stopped. Smoke told me to stay here while he went to get the surprise. I placed my hands on my hips and started tapping my foot. I was beginning to get an attitude because I didn't like surprises and this blindfold wasn't the business.

"Ight ma, take it off!" Smoke said.

"Finally," I sassed.

I took the blindfold off my eyes, and once I did, the first thing I saw was an olive green drop top. I ain't know what kind of car it was, but it was beautiful. I walked over to the car and looked at the inside. It was all cream-colored leather with my named stitched in the head of the seats.

"This ain't mine," I said in shock.

"This shit is all yours." Smoke told me. "You like it?"

"Do I like it? I love it. It's so pretty and it's got my name in the headrest."

"Check out the license plate."

"I went to the back of the car and looked at the license plate. It read Mrs. Smoke."

"Shaheem, I don't know what to say." I started to cry because this was all too much.

"You don't have to say shit. I'm doing this cause you deserve it. This a bomb ass surprise, right? I bet ya ass like surprises now."

"This is more than a surprise. This is the most meaningful thing anyone has ever done to me. Growing up when my birthday would come around I used to always think my mother was going to surprise with a cake when I came home from school. Come to find out she wasn't trying to surprise me, she just didn't care about my birthday. After a while, I stopped looking for a surprise and started to hate them. But this...this is beautiful Shaheem. Thank you."

I jumped into his arms not even thinking if he would catch me or not. Thankfully, he did, and I wrapped my legs around his waist and gave him the most meaningful kiss that I could. He kissed me back with twice the intensity and even more devotion.

"I love you, Promyse," he whispered, ending the kiss.

I was at a loss for words because I didn't think we were there yet. I mean our feelings for each other were there, but love? I wasn't sure if I loved him. I couldn't just leave him hanging after he brought me a car.

"I lov..."

"Shut the fuck up cause we both know you're not there yet. You don't have to say that shit just cause I did. My feelings are different from yours, and I found what I thought I never needed. You still got time to grow and shit. When you tell me you love me, I want it to be real and not because you feel obligated to tell me it back."

"Do you really love me?"

I didn't believe that Smoke loved me because how could someone like him love someone like me. We were nothing alike. I struggled most of my life and was still struggling. Smoke, on the other hand, was born into money and even had money passed down to him. Being with someone like me was one thing, but to love me was to know me and understand my issues.

"I know it seems crazy, but I'm deadass when I say that shit to you lil ma. You're everything I never knew I needed and then some. Believe me when I say it cause my words are true, ma.

"I believe you." I smiled.

"Ight enough of the soft shit cause you got ya nigga soundin' like a straight bitch. Come out to the front with me so that I can get something out the car."

"Okay."

We started walking towards the front of the dealership when it dawned on me that he brought me a car when I couldn't drive.

"I can't believe you brought me a car, and I can't drive." I was looking at him when he stopped me in mid-stride.

"I can teach you," I heard someone say from behind me. The voice was familiar, but it couldn't be who I thought it was. The person I thought it was didn't speak clearly like that because her voice was mostly gone. The person I thought it was would never volunteer to teach me how to drive because she didn't give a fuck about me. Nah, it couldn't be who I thought it was.

"Turn around, Promyse," Smoke said with a smile on his face.

"Smoke is that my mother behind me?" I whispered so only he could hear me.

"You gotta turn around ma and find out."

"Smoke, I'm not ready to see her just yet."

"No one is ever really ready to see the person that hurt them the most, but at some point, you gotta rip off the band-aid and deal with the pain. You got this, and whenever you feel like you don't, I'll be right next to you."

I nodded my head at him cause he was right. I just had to deal with the pain and not let the pain overcome me. I let out a deep breath then slowly turned around. I was looking at the ground at first, but I slowly raised my eyes until they connected with my mother's. She didn't look like the woman I remembered. She wasn't all frail and wearing dirty clothes. Her hair wasn't matted to her hair either. She looked like an older version of me. She looked good and clean.

"Ma," I said with tears blurring my vision.

"Shhh baby, you don't have to say anything," she said, coming over to me. She wrapped her arms around me and told me how sorry she was for all that she put me through. All she kept saying was that she was sorry.

Hearing her say that to me was like hearing that I won a million dollars. This was all I ever wanted since I realized that my mother was hooked on drugs. This was the moment I've been waiting for my whole life, and I was finally getting. I was finally going to have the mother I always wanted, and it was all because of Smoke. He just kept doing things that proved to me he that was the one. There was no way he was brought into my world to cause me hell cause all he been doing was giving me heaven on earth. If I wasn't certain about overseeing his trap before, I was beyond certain now. It was the least I could do after all he's done for me.

Chapter Fourteen

KHYREE

"Fuck ma, ease up doing that shit!" I groaned.

"You like it papi, so enjoy it cause ya other bitch can't do what I do."

"Man!" I stressed.

I reached to the left snatched up a pillow and placed it over her face. I was tryin' to bust a nut not hear how her pussy was better than Paulie's was. I kept stroking her shit showing no mercy. A nigga was angry fuckin'. On God, I was tryin' to knock her pussy the fuck out.

"Just like that, papi! Give it to me just like that!" she screamed. Her screams were exotic and pissing me off even more. They were like ecstasy to my ears, and I knew I wasn't gon' be able to leave her alone after getting a sample of what her pussy do.

Her shit was dripping wet and tight as fuck. What made it better was she knew how to use her pussy muscles. Her shit went from being tight to suffocating with no effort at all. My head was spinning, and I couldn't hold out anymore. I hit her shit a couple more times then released a load into the condom. I slid out of her and fell on the bed lying on my back.

"I know I told you when we first met that all I needed was thirty minutes and I could change your life, but that hour and a half did wonders on my life," she purred.

I smirked at her and watched as she took the condom off and brought it up to her lips. I looked on interested cause wasn't no way she was about to do a shot with my kids.

"You want some?" she offered.

"Nah I'm good. Do ya thing."

"Cool."

She opened her mouth, and my seeds slowly slid down her throat. The shit was nasty and a turn on at the same time. That was some freaky nasty shit, but a nigga was into it. Ole girl got out of bed and started putting her clothes on. See, I was into this type of shit, a chick that knew her place and played her position well.

"Damn ma, it's like that. You just gon' suck up a nigga's seeds then dip?" I asked playing around with her.

"You and I both know that in an hour or even thirty minutes you're going to feel bad about what you did. I, on the other hand. enjoyed all of last night and this morning."

"You weren't fuckin' with the afternoon?"

"I especially enjoyed that, but it's my time to go. I don't want to overstay my welcome cause I'm trying to see you again."

"Look Oliv...."

"You don't have to say anything because I already know what it is. You got a girl at home that you love, and this was a one-time thing. I get it, but what I'm saying to you is if you ever just need to release some stress I'm here. What I will say is you need to stop fuckin' with them minors and get you a grown woman. I would never stress to the point that it drives you into the arms of another woman. When you're ready to upgrade your life on some grown shit, holla at me cause I can be a main chick as well as a side chick." She winked at me then grabbed her bag and started heading towards the hotel door. Before she walked out, she turned towards me with a smirk on her face.

"Oh and before I forget my name isn't Oliva, it's Mercy."

I laughed when she closed the door cause I didn't know where I got Oliva from. When I first met her at the club with Fame and them she told me her name, but the shit didn't stick cause she wasn't nothing but eye candy. Her ass was fat, and I didn't mind it resting on my lap. When I went back to the club after leaving the crib, I ran into her again. One thing led to another, and we ended up in a room. I was sure she told me her name, but again that shit didn't matter. She was a stress reliever.

I couldn't lie tho her pussy was beyond amazing. I thought Paulie shit was elite, but Mercy was giving her a run for her money. Even with her having good pussy there was no way I was wifing her. Shawty was too much of a freak, and I was sure she ran the same game on me that she did on other niggas. I ran up in shawty with a condom, but after that shit Lola was talking, I was taking my ass to be tested tomorrow morning just to make sure. These women out here were scandalous as fuck, and I wasn't trying to get caught up and bring anything back to Paulie.

Speaking of Paulie, guilt started to sink in. She didn't deserve to get cheated on, but the way she came at me last night fucked me all up. I couldn't think right. The pain from what happened to my parents replayed in my head as I drove around trying to cool off. My mother's blood on my hands reappeared as I gripped the steering wheel last night. A nigga was suffering all over again. I needed something to take my mind off it all and Mercy just so happened to be that something. I fucked up, and I was gon' be man enough to let Paulie know what happened. I wasn't fond of secret and hiding shit, so the best thing to do was to come clean.

I got out of bed and grabbed my phone off the desk that was in the room. I powered it on then headed for the bathroom. I turned the shower on then sat on the toilet to take a shit. The first message to come through was from Paulie. It was basically telling me that she would be here for me and shit like that. I replied telling her that we needed to talk and that I would be home within the hour. She hit me right back like she was sitting by her phone waiting for me to respond. She said she would be there waiting for me and for me to drive safe.

I ain't know how things were going to play out between Paulie and I. I had violated our relationship by sleeping with Mercy. I wasn't gon' say that I hoped Paulie forgave me cause maybe it wasn't meant for her to forgive me. I wanted Paulie, and I knew she was the one for me deep down, but just cause she was for me didn't mean she was for me right now. If I cared for Paulie as much as I thought I did, I wouldn't have fucked her over the way that I did.

$ $ $

Pulling up to the crib, I sat in the car for a minute trying to get my thoughts together. After some thought, I realized that right now wasn't the time for Paulie and I. We were two different people in two different places. She was fueled by emotion while I tried to keep my emotions at bay. The argument we had led me to do some foul shit that felt good. Paulie wasn't the only one to blame cause I had the opportunity to be open with her. Instead of letting her in, I locked her out, and this was the result of that. We were both gon' have to take responsibility for the parts we played in our demise.

"Might as well get this shit over with," I said aloud and stepped out the car.

I walked into the house and was hit with the aroma of food and the sweet sound of Beyoncé singing her heart out about being dangerously in love. I was caught off guard cause Paulie been stuck in that room for a week. The last thing I expected to come home to was a home-cooked meal.

"Hey baby, you're home!" She smiled, coming over and giving me a hug and kiss.

"What made you cook?" I asked with a raised eyebrow. "You tryin' to kill a nigga?" I wasn't serious when I asked that, but by the time we finished our talk, I wouldn't be surprised if she deadass tried to kill me.

"I wanted to do something nice for you. I've been in a funk lately, and because of that, I ended up saying some things to you that I know hurt you. I'm young and naïve when it comes to dating. No that's not an excuse, but it's the truth. I'm going to make mistakes and say things that I shouldn't say. I'm not saying that making them is ok. What I'm saying is I need you to understand and have some patience with me. Things might not be how we want them to be, but trust me if you just stick it out with me I swear it will be worth it. I need you to know that I'm worth all the trouble I cause."

Her words sunk in and if I said they didn't touch me, I would be lying. I knew things were gonna be hard because of her age; I just didn't think it would be like this. Walking in the house, I didn't expect all of this. I ain't know exactly what I expected, but I knew it wasn't what I was getting. Paulie was womaning up to her shit and letting me know that things weren't gonna always be all bad. She just wanted me to stick it out through the bad times. Instead of being a solid nigga, I fucked up. I cheated on my shawty and looking at her be vulnerable and open there was no way I could break her heart.

"Khyree, I need you to say something. The silence is killing me. If you're still mad, that's fine, but I need you to say something. Yell, scream, or hit me." She paused for a minute and thought about what she just said. "I don't literally mean hit me, but you know what I mean. I just need you to say or do something, baby." She looked at me searching my eyes for a sign that I was there with her.

I wasn't big on lying, but a nigga was about to omit the truth. I would hit Mercy up tomorrow to make sure she kept shit on the hush.

"When my father killed my mother, he scarred me for life. He had me scared as hell to get into a relationship because I never wanted to do to my shawty what he did to my moms. To stop myself from hurting any chick I ever rocked with, I never let things get serious. I fucked and kept it pushing."

"Khy, I don't want to hear about the woman you slept with," she said, interrupting me.

"I know, but hear me out. Most chicks thought I was ducking them cause I was a playa or doing that typical street shit. I let them run with that cause it was better than them knowing the truth, but when it came to you shit changed. Don't get me wrong I stepped to you on some fuck shit. It wasn't until we really started talking that I saw you for who you were. You made a nigga want to try something new and even through the fear of turning into my father was there it didn't matter. I ain't give a fuck about being that nigga cause I knew you were going to keep me on my toes. The way you had my ass calling you every night and texting you everyday let me know you weren't gon' let a nigga fall off. You're my strength without even knowing it. The way you're in my corner is the way I'ma be in yours when you fuck up. That shit you said is dead and in the past. We ain't gotta talk about it or dwell on it."

"I mean I know I'm popping and what not, but you're just gonna let me off the hook like that?"

"You ain't the only one to blame. If I would've told you bout my parents when you asked, then you would've known better. I held that information from you, and because I did that, you said some fucked up shit. You apologized, and I'm over it; no need to discuss it anymore." I grabbed her in my arms and kissed her on the forehead.

"If you ever want to talk about your parents I'm here."

"Ight, I got you. Is that it tho cause you got it smellin' right in here and a nigga hungry."

"So greedy." She giggled. "I do have one thing to ask of you, and then we can eat."

"What's that?"

"From this point no more secrets. Tell me all your dreams and fears. I want to know it all and then some. I don't want there to be a thing about you that I don't know and vice versa."

"In due time, you'll learn everything you need to know. In the meantime let's enjoy our time together."

A nigga was feeling like shit but what could I do. Her mom's kicked her out cause of my ass. Telling her I cheated seemed like the right thing to do at first, but shit changed. I was gonna have to go against one of my rules in order to protect her heart. I was good with that. I just need baby girl by my side on some forever type shit.

Chapter Fifteen

FAME

"How did things go?" I asked as I leaned back in my chair.

I was at one of my apartments out in Jersey. It felt good to be back home. Going to New York from time to time was cool, but I was out there for way too long. Saigon was so into ole girl that the nigga had us out there for about two weeks. I could've easily left and came back home, but I wasn't the type to leave my nigga hangin'. I ain't understand his obsession with ole girl, but who was I to knock it or judge. I just hoped he played it safe. The last hoe he tried to save ended up being dirty as fuck. She was on some get back shit for a nigga that ain't even want her bum ass. Needless to say, she and her nigga are both gone may they souls rest in hell for eternity.

"He went for it, and I secured the deal. You should already know that you don't have to ask. When I get the key, I put it in the hole and lock that muthafucker."

"I don't know bout all that key shit but good. Make sure you stay in contact with his ass. Something seems off bout them niggas. I need to make sure we're breaking bread with solid niggas."

When it came to this drug shit, I was super caution. I didn't plan on doing jail time for someone else's fuck up. I made sure to make sure everyone we sold to was the real thing. Wasn't no fakes in our crew and that's how it was going to stay.

"What's the point in looking into them or watching them if they already down with the crew? They know of your operation and shit, so if they were on some dirty shit, they would know everything they needed to know."

"They ain't down with the crew. They're moving ¼ of the weight they could be moving. As far as them knowing our operation, they don't know shit. They know what we want them to know," I corrected her.

"I still don't understand the point in all of this, but as long as the money keeps coming in, I'm good."

"Good to know. You can dismiss ya self now."

"Rude muthafucker!" She snickered. "You know if you let me I can fix that attitude of yours."

"Ma, you done fixed way too many attitudes for my blood. You can't get close to a nigga like me. I don't do thot."

"If a bitch wasn't a thot who would do all the work you throwing my way. Just cause I like sex doesn't mean I'm a thot. I'm open about my sexuality."

"Money will have a lot of bitches doing just about anything. You ain't special, ma. Chicks that are open and comfortable about their sexuality and sexual activity comes a dime a dozen."

"Yea okay, Fame. You and I both know that's bullshit. Without me, shit would fall apart. Snakes would be all in your grass if it weren't for me. I won't say much just keep fronting on the kid and watch what happens." She smiled standing up.

"Sit the fuck back down," I told her as calmly as I could.

"You just told me to leave, and now you want me to stay. Daddy, I'ma need you to make up your mind, or I can make it up for you." She walked around my desk and pushed my chair back.

She quickly straddled my lap and licked her lips. My right hand crept up her leg and then went up her back. My hand didn't stop moving until I had a hand full of the weave she was rocking. I wrapped it around my hand then yanked her head back not giving a fuck if I snapped her neck or not.

"Listen when I tell you this shit and listen good. Don't ever in ya thot ass life threaten me or form a sentence that makes me think you're threatening me.

You're fucking disposable, and it's nothing to dispose of you. You don't keep snakes out a nigga's grass. I do that shit on my own. The most you do is fuck a nigga to see where his head at. You're a pawn in this game of chess. You're the least special piece on the whole game board. Play with me if you want, and things can get hectic for a thot like you. Now get the fuck out before I break your fuckin' neck!" I let her hair go then pushed her ass off my lap.

She fell to the floor making a thud sound. I pulled my phone out and started scrolling as she got up and left out my office. I hated putting my hands on females, but sometimes that shit was needed. Let me correct myself I wasn't putting my hands on females cause my mother taught me better than that. I would slap a thot or rough one up in a New York minute. Those types of females didn't give a fuck about their own lives, so why the fuck would I? I didn't play when it came to certain shit, and shawty knew that. Where she was getting all that mouth from was beyond me, but that shit was gon' get her ass fucked up.

"My nigga why I just saw ya girl rushing out of here cursing ya ass out? What you do to her?" Saigon asked, laughing.

"I ain't do shit to her dumb ass. I had to yoke her ass up for the shit she was saying. She came in her talkin' slick like she got it like that. You already know I don't play when it comes to that smart mouth shit."

"Nigga, you can't blame no one but yo self for the way she's acting. You let her handle all these niggas like she's your right hand or some shit. In her eyes, she's on a pedestal that can't be touched. I told you before and I'ma say it one last time, you need to let shawty go. She's going to cause more problems than she's solving."

"Fuck that; she's good at what she does. Whenever she causes a problem that's too big for me to handle, then she will get dealt with. In the meantime, I'm rocking with shawty cause she been on her shit."

"You sure you ain't checkin' for her? I ain't know you to keep a problematic chick or nigga around?"

"Nigga, don't try and play on that shit. You know I don't love these hoes, the hoes love the kid. That's you that be on that captain save a hoe bullshit."

"Get the fuck outta here. What hoe am I lovin'?"

"Smoke's girl." I laughed.

Saigon always played shit smooth when it came to the chicks he dated. For someone reason, he never wanted to admit the obvious. I ain't know if it was his pride or what, but he would never admit to fuckin' with a hoe. A chick could've just hopped off the next nigga's dick, and he would swear up and down she wasn't a hoe. I ain't understand the shit, and if it were anyone else,

I would've swore they were bitch made. Saigon was different. There wasn't an ounce of bitch in his blood. He was as ruthless as the rest of us, yet he had a soft spot for these hoes.

"She ain't that nigga's girl, and she ain't a hoe."

"Yeah, ight. I don't care what she is, she's with that nigga, and you need to fall back off that."

"I can't leave someone alone that I'm not fuckin' with. All we have is conversation. Ain't shit goin' on between the two of us, and if there was, you could bet your money on it that she would be here with me and not with that lame ass nigga."

"How you calling that nigga a lame when you said he reminded you of us when we were younger?"

"Business-wise he reminds me of myself. On the personal tip, that nigga ain't shit."

"Chalk that shit up to whatever you want. I keep telling you bout falling for these Cinderella types. You need to leave that shit alone."

"The fuck is a Cinderella type?"

"You know the chicks that have it hard but go out and find them a baller. They act hard to get and then give in all to go on and live a lavish life they don't deserve."

"What makes you think shawty don't deserve the good life?"

"Unless she's working for the shit, she doesn't deserve

it. Any chick that's not trying to better herself from jump ain't gon' do shit but drain you down the line. That's what's wrong with the chicks in this generation. They think they can suck and fuck their way into the good life and shit will be sweet. No one is out here working for theirs anymore. The shit is sad as fuck that's why I ain't wifing shit out here."

I ain't have time for a chick that was only coming for mine. She needed to have her own before I became a thought in her mind. I refused to finance a chick that wasn't doing shit. I wanted that independent type chick that Ne-yo was making songs about. It was either I was gon' get the type of chick I wanted, or these hoes were just gon' keep getting the dick.

"I hear what you saying, but I got this. I learned from my past mistakes, and I'm not bout to fuck shit up again."

"I'm just tryin' to look out for you."

"I 'preciate that, but I got this. I don't need assistance cause I know what I'm doing. I'm not stressing shawty. I'll have her soon enough. It's just a matter of time at this point."

"Say less, my nigga. Did ya pops hit you tellin' you to come through?"

"Yeah Dragon's ole ass hit me. I told him I would come through after I got up with you."

Saigon and I kicked it a lil' while longer before going

to see our fathers. They wanted to holla at us about something they thought could be beneficial. I ain't know what they had up their sleeves, but I was down for just about anything at this point. Money was my only focus since I ain't have a shawty of my own. I liked to act like I ain't need a chick, but truth be told, I wanted me a lil' baby to come home to every night.

She couldn't be just any ordinary chick from around the way. Nah shawty, had to be the female version of me. She needed to have her head on straight and be focused. Money driven but not money hungry. For me to wife a chick, she had to have it all. Looking for someone who had it all was probably where I kept falling short. My pops told me a long time ago that I would never find a chick that was a hundred. The chick I fall for would only be eighty percent of what I was looking for. That other twenty percent that they were lacking was the temptation of what I would find in another bitch. I wasn't trying to hear that shit then, and I'm damn sure not trying to hear that shit now. A nigga was willing to be a chick's hundred percent. I might've even been feeling generous and gave her an extra ten percent to fall in love with. The point was if I was out here giving a chick hundred percent, she needed to give me the same. Settling wasn't gon' happen ever for a nigga. I was either gon' get what I wanted or not fuck with anyone on a serious level at all.

Chapter Sixteen

SAIGON

Walking into my father's house, I felt a cold chill run over my body. I loved my pops on some real shit, but comin' to his crib wasn't something I did often. Every time I walked through the door, the cold feeling I was feeling now would wash over me. I told my pops back in the day he needed to sell the house and get a new one, but he wasn't trying to hear it. He refused to sell the house cause it reminded him of her. It was the last thing of her that he had, and he wasn't going to part with it no matter who was uncomfortable in the house.

Just thinking about her had tears ready to fall from my eyes. A nigga was far from being soft, but when it came to her soft was the only thing a nigga knew how to be. She was my heart and my queen. She was the woman who carried me for ten months and had a C-section just to save my life and give me life. She was the first woman I ever loved. She was everything to me, and when I was supposed to be her hero, I fell short. I was supposed to be her savior when my father wasn't around, and a nigga fell short. I just fall short. I let her down, and because of that, her death was on my hands.

"Aye, you ight? You got that far off look in ya eyes," Fame said.

"Yeah, I'm straight."

"You sure? You not trippin' off that shit I was talkin' bout ole girl, right?"

"Ain't no one sweatin' that shit. I'm good."

"Ight."

Fame was my brother, and there wasn't much about me that he didn't know. When it came to what happened to my mom, I kept it to myself. I was too ashamed to bring myself to talk about it with anyone. I failed my mother, and that wasn't something I could come back from. I was sixteen when my mother's life was taken away from me. She died in my arms, and the fucked up thing is I replayed that moment so much in my mind that I could probably reenact the whole situation. That's how fucked up I was behind it.

We were going to the fish market cause my mother wanted to have a seafood feast for my father. She was always doing little things like cooking my father's favorite meals just to show him how much she cared. With my father being heavy in the streets and spending very little time at home, my mother was the one to teach me how to drive. That day I was having a lesson and driving to the fish market. We were sitting at a red light talkin' about some chick I was into at the time. A black Toyota pulled up next to us and started bussin'.

They didn't bother putting silencers on their guns. They let their shits ring off like they wanted the world to know what they just did. Instead of speeding off when the guns started going off, I sat there frozen watching each bullet enter my mother's body. I didn't move until the black Toyota pulled off. I snatched my mother up and watched her life slip from her body as her blood stained my white t-shirt and blue jeans. That was the first time a nigga experienced heartbreak.

If I would've known back then what I know now, then shit would've gone down differently. I ain't think nothing of that raggedy Toyota pulling up next to us. My father kept the street life from me until I was about seventeen. He didn't want me involved in that life until I was of age. That night fucked up my head and changed me forever. My father combed the streets of Jersey and New York looking for the muthafuckers who did it, but no one was talkin' and wasn't shit shakin'. After a while, my father put what happened to my mother behind him. I kept that shit near my heart and was still on the search for them niggas.

Fame thought I was out here saving hoes and shit for the hell of it. I could admit I had a thing for women who were in distress. I wasn't proud of that cause it fucked me over. Truth be told I was trying to make up for not saving my mother. I figured if I could make just one person's life better than I would be able to let go of the hurt. Emmy was supposed to be that person, but her ass was on some other shit. What she did cut a nigga deep and for a minute, I wasn't tryin' to fuck with anyone. I won't say seeing Promyse changed that, but seeing her on that stage lit something in my soul. Her innocence shined through that night while the hurt in her eyes tried to dim it. I wouldn't say she needed saving, but she damn sure needed someone cause the one she had wasn't doing shit for her. I wasn't the type to steal a nigga's chick. At first I was gon' let shit rock, but that nigga Smoke ain't know what he had in Promyse. I ain't really know what she was about, but a nigga saw her potential and that shit was more than I could say for half the chicks running around here.

"Sai, you ight? You don't hear us talkin' to you?" my father asked, looking in my direction. I ain't even realize they were having a whole conversation.

"I'm good. What happened?"

"These old ass niggas called us over here to play one on one," Fame said.

"Old man, who you think you bout to beat in ball?" I joked

"Young nigga don't get it twisted; you got your skills from me."

"Yeah ight, let you tell it. Rich, you gon' let this old nigga talk you out of your money?"

"He ain't talkin' me out of shit. I know what I'm good

at, and ball ain't one of them. While his old ass makes a fool of himself, I'ma be on the grill." Fame's father laughed.

"Damn, after all the years we got in you just gon' sell ya boy out like that?"

"Nigga, you know ya old ass can't play anymore. I don't even know why you tryin' to go against these niggas. Shit, if they weren't trappin' they'll be ballin'."

"Straight truth," Fame cosigned. "Hol' up I thought y'all wanted us to roll through cause y'all had a way for us to make more money?"

"Y'all make more than enough money. The fuck y'all need more for?" Rich said.

"A nigga can't ever have too much money. Money makes the world go around," Fame told him.

"Money ain't what's important in the world, family is. And with the way you niggas movin', family don't mean shit to the two of you. We ain't seen y'all in a month of Sundays," my father said.

"Pops, you wildin'. You already know family means everything to me, but shit don't stop cause we want to spend time with the fam. Y'all know how stressful shit be with what we got going on. We don't have the luxury of chillin' when we want like y'all two," I told him.

"I ain't saying be up under us every chance you get. What I'm saying is not many guys can say their fathers are in their lives. Be proud that y'all got two fathers who give a fuck about y'all and want to spend time. Shit, I'm cool with a phone call, but a nigga can't even get that," Rich said, looking at Fame.

"Damn Pops, don't call me out like that."

"I'ma call you out when you're doing wrong, and right now you doing wrong."

"Ight my bad, I'll do better," Fame told him.

"Sai, you're my only child and all I got left. If you don't want to be bothered with ya pops then make some grandchildren. I'll be straight and won't need to see ya ass."

"I'm too young for kids right now."

"Better to have them young than when you old and can't bust a move," my father joked.

"I'll come around more and spend time ight old man."

"Cool with me. Bring ya ass on. I ain't forget bout takin' ya money. Fame, bring ya ass too," my father said, getting up and heading outside.

Fame and I looked at each other and then busted out laughing. We headed outside to play ball. I heard everything my father was saying. I got he wanted to spend more time, but being in this house just wasn't the same. It ain't feel like a home cause the woman who made it a home was gone.

Chapter Seventeen

PROMYSE

"What you mean Secret is home? How are you feeling?" Paulie asked.

We were sitting outside waiting for Lola to come through so that I could show them my car. I've been MIA for the past couple of days due to me trying to get comfortable being around my mother. I wasn't used to the clean version of her. It was like she was a whole new person. Every morning she got up and made breakfast and asked me what was going in my life. She wanted to know about all the things she's missed while she was in rehab and all the things she missed when she didn't give a fuck. I didn't think I was going to be excited to be around my mother when she came back. I thought everything she's done to me was going to scar me and have me resent her. But, looking at the clean her had me forgetting all the bullshit that she put me through. It gave me hope that we could have that mother and daughter relationship I wanted my whole life.

"Honestly, I love having her back. I mean we still have a lot to work through, but I finally have the mother I've wanted."

"Damn, I can't believe she's back let alone clean. I ain't think I was ever going to see that day."

"Thanks," I said sarcastically.

"I didn't mean it like that I'm just saying. Secret had a lot that she had to work on. She's only been gone about a month maybe a month and a half. I think it's going to take longer than that to slay her demons."

"I know she's not perfect, and she still has a lot of work, I'm just happy that she's back and clean."

"If you're happy then I'm happy. You deserve to have a mother in your life that cares about you."

"Thank you, Paulie."

She smiled at me then pulled me in for a hug. I hugged her back feeling like my life was finally where I wanted and needed it to be. I had my mother, a boyfriend that thought the world of me, and friends that would go to the end of the earth for me. I was up right now and planned on staying this way for a while.

"Where the hell is Lola? Her ass is always late but gets mad when someone keeps her ass waiting," Paulie sassed.

"Here she comes right now," I told her, nodding in Lola's direction.

We stood up and meet Lola halfway. It made no sense for her to come our way when we needed to go the back of the projects cause that's where Smoke parked my car.

"Wassup bitches!" Lola greeted us.

"Nothing much we were just talking about Promyse's mom being home," Paulie told her.

"Secret's back? Wait, when did she leave?"

I forgot that Lola wasn't around when Smoke had my mom sent to rehab. I was on the fence about letting Lola back in my life cause I still didn't trust her. She seemed to had let go of all the Smoke jealousy, but I wasn't sure.

"She went to rehab and came back a few days ago."

"Well alright, Secret. It's about time her ass came to her sense and got clean. I was tired of looking at her be a mess."

"Lola really?" Paulie asked.

I just shook my head and kept it pushing. This was exactly why I wasn't sure about letting her back into my life.

"What? I was just being honest. All three of us knows she was a mess. If she's clean now, then there is no need to dance around how she was a mess in the past. You don't dwell on things like that. You laugh at it later and move on."

"That may be how you handle things, but it's not how I do it. I done beat your ass once this summer, don't make me do it again," I gritted, looking at her.

"Woah! Chill out Promyse cause I don't want no heat. I'm sorry I said anything."

"Good." I turned back around and kept it pushing.

I heard Paulie and Lola talking, but couldn't really hear what they were saying because I was still pissed off. Since Lola wanted to be a bitch, I was going to be a bitch too. I was tired of her walking all over me and think she could say whatever she wanted. If she was going to be back in this group, then I was going to put her in her place. She wasn't the poppin' one in the group in anymore.

"Why are we coming back here when none of us has a car? I thought we were going out to eat?"

"We are going out, and one of us does have a car." I smiled.

"Paulie, Khy brought your ass a car?" she asked excitedly as hell.

"Girl, Khy ain't buy me no damn car."

"Then who got a car?"

"I do!" I smiled, jumping on the trunk of my car.

Lola's mouth dropped to the floor, and Paulie's eyes lit up. I smiled at Lola cause I knew she was feeling real envious of me. I never wanted any of my friends to be jealous of me, but it felt good to see Lola shocked that I had something she didn't.

"Bitch, when did you get this and why am I just finding out about it?" Paulie questioned.

"That day I left you in my house, Smoke came and got me. He brought me to the dealership and surprised me with this and my mother. It was the cutest thing I've ever seen," I gushed.

"I can't believe he got you a car and ya ass can't even drive." Paulie laughed. I laughed along with her and watched Lola from the corner of my eye. She was looking at the car with a semi-sour look on her face.

"Why is your face lookin' like you just sucked on a lemon, Lola?"

"Girl, no one is looking sour. I'm just mesmerized. This is my dream car."

"I don't even know what kind of car it is but it's so pretty, and the seats are engraved with my name."

"It's an Audi A5 Cabriolet."

"How you know that? You're into cars?" Paulie asked her.

"No, but this is my dream car. I read about it in one of those urban books and Googled it. Once I saw what it looked like, I fell in love. Can I drive it? I mean you can't drive so we might as well, and it doesn't make sense to take the train or a cab to the restaurant."

"Smoke doesn't want me to let anyone drive it, but I think I can make an exception." I smiled.

"Toss me the keys cause I'm bout to glide all in this bitch." Lola smiled.

"Here Paulie." I tossed her the keys then hopped off the car.

"Wait what?" Lola asked.

"I've been in a car that you drove before, and you drive reckless. I don't need my new baby getting fucked up," I lied. I was being real childish, but I didn't care because she deserved it. She could chalk it up to pay back for the shit she said about my mother.

"If Smoke doesn't want anyone driving the car, I wouldn't feel right driving it. You know that nigga is crazy. The last thing I need is him trying to ride down on me."

"Paulie, you're fine. Come on before we're late for my meeting," I told them, getting in on the passenger side.

"What meeting?" Paulie asked as she and Lola got in the car.

"Smoke set up a lunch meeting between me and the two girls that will be working in Harlem with me. Their names are Bliss and Jiya. I didn't want to go alone."

"You know I'm down for whatever. I just don't want no parts in what you got going on," Paulie said, pulling off.

"What do you have going on? Y'all talking in code like you don't want me to know the business." Lola sassed.

I looked at her through the rearview trying to see what her intentions were. I hated that Lola was so hard to read. I couldn't tell if she was really for me or just trying to use me or something. Telling her what I had going on could hurt me depending on what she did with the information.

"I know I fucked up in the past, but I'm telling you that I'm over that," she said.

"Smoke has me helping him with a spot out in Harlem. I won't be doing too much he just wants me to meet with these two chicks."

"Aw shit, let me find out Promyse is shedding her good girl skin."

"I'm not shedding anything. I'm just trying to help my man out."

"I hear that," she said. "Well, what restaurant are we going to cause I'm hungry as hell, and I need to look at the menu ahead of time?"

"Olive Garden," I told her.

"Cool."

I thought Lola would've dug a little deeper, but she let the conversation go quickly, and she didn't judge me or say anything smart. I was impressed. I may have flossed on her when it came to my car as get back, but I wanted our friendship to work. The three of us been friends for the longest and been through a lot. They were there for me when I had no one else. We've had tough times, but they didn't outweigh the good times. I didn't want either one of them out of my life. I didn't have a problem letting Lola go, but if I didn't have to kick her out my life, then I wasn't going to. The same people that were there for me when I struggled, I wanted to be the same people that were with me while I was winning.

Chapter Eighteen
BISS

"I don't even know why we agreed to meet with this bitch. I thought you said they were giving us full control to do things how we wanted them done? I'm not feeling having someone supervise us like we don't know what we're doing. This is bullshit, and I'm not for it," Jiya complained. I rolled my eyes hard as hell at her.

"You can get up and walk right out that door if this ain't where you want to be."

"I'm not saying this isn't where I want to be. I'm just saying that I didn't agree to this bullshit. We're not new to this, and we shouldn't be treated as such. We deserve more respect than this. Matter of fact why ain't you mad? This is bullshit, and you know it, Bliss."

"Jiya, what the fuck you want me to do? I'm not the one in charge, those niggas are. I don't have no choice but to follow their lead."

"Bliss, you have a choice, and I'm telling you right now this is the wrong one."

"Then let me make the mistake cause I'm not walking away. I need the money. I'm tired of getting the short end of the stick. I'm trying to see that money these niggas be talkin' bout in their songs. The type of money that can take me from a small ass two-bedroom apartment to a mansion up in someone's hills. I'm trying to get everything I deserve on my own. I want Blessing to grow up and know that she doesn't need a nigga for shit. I need her to know that if her mother can get out here and make good money, then she can do the same. Granted I don't want her doing the same shit I'm doing, but the lesson remains the same."

"You're talking about Blessing like I want my god baby to be dependent on some no good nigga. You should know me better than that. I want nothing but the best for you and Blessing. Hell, I even want the best for myself, but I'm letting you know now this right here isn't the move. Look at it this way, why them niggas didn't just put ole girl in the spot from the jump? Why now just bring her in when they had sit-downs with the both of us and never said anything about us having a supervisor. Something ain't right about this shit."

"Well, what do you want me to do?" I asked her. What she was saying made sense, but I wasn't going to just up and leave without seeing who shawty was. I needed to know who was that important that I needed a supervisor.

"My right mind is telling me that we need to leave, but I already know you're not going to do that. So we don't have no choice but to ride this out. I'm letting you know now tho if this bitch says or does anything that makes me feel uncomfortable, I'm shooting her on sight. That bitch can blink and if it throws me off her ass is getting shot."

"Jiya, you can't be serious. You're really going to shoot ole girl in a public place."

"I'm serious as hell. I will cap that bitch right in her big toe." She laughed.

I shook my head because on God my cousin ain't have no common sense. I laughed with her then took a sip of my drink. Looking at my Michael Kors watch, I realized that ole girl was late. That was her first strike. If I hated anything, it was my time being wasted. It was bad enough that some random bitch was going to be clocking my moves. For her to show up late to the meeting showed she didn't need to be clocking shit but a clock.

" I should shoot that bitch off GP. Her ass is late as fuck."

"Hol' up I think this is her." I nodded towards the hostess as three girls walked in.

The hostess looked my way then brought them over. Taking in these chicks, they looked no older than eighteen. Smoke couldn't have been serious. There was no way I was letting some high school bitch dictate how my shit was going to be ran.

"This nigga is a fuckin' cradle robber," Jiya whispered before they got to the table.

"Hey, you must be Bliss and Jiya." The chick speaking stuck her hand out as if I was going to shake it. I looked at Jiya, and she looked at me. Without a word being said we already knew how this was going to go down.

"I'm Bliss, that's Jiya. Who are you?"

"I'm Promyse, and these are my friends Lola and Paulie," she introduced.

"What are they doing here? Smoke said you were coming solo."

"I was out when Smoke told me to come meet you, so I just brought them along. We're having lunch so I figured we could all eat together."

"That's your first fuck up," I told her.

"Excuse me."

"You heard what I said that's your first fuck up. Never bring outsiders to business meetings. No matter how casual a meeting is, the only people who need to be in attendance is the ones handling business."

"Oh, you don't have to worry about them snitching or anything like that."

I laughed to myself because this was comical. Not only were these chicks still sucking on Similac, but the one who was running things didn't know what she was about to get herself into.

"Have a seat so we can get this started." Jiya moved from the opposite side and came to sit next to me.

The three baby musketeers sat down, and that's when things got interesting. They all sat down and refused to look us in the eye. Well, let me correct that, Promyse and Paulie refused to look us in the eye. The other chick Lola didn't have a problem looking at us. I respected her the most just because she didn't let us intimidate her.

"Pick y'all heads up we're not the table," Jiya sassed. "Not to be rude or nothing but the two of them got to go. I let them take a seat for a second to relax their feet cause I know you bitches ain't driving. But, if we getting to business, they can't be here. I don't discuss business in front of people I don't know."

"You can watch how you're talking to us because we're not your children!" Paulie snapped right back. Something about her voice sounded familiar, but I couldn't place it.

"I already said they're cool, so I don't know what the problem is."

"I heard what you said, and I don't give a fuck. I don't know them so they don't need to be here. The only person who can assure I have nothing to worry about is my cousin and me. Not you or these two bitches are going to change that. And as far as I can see y'all might as well be my children. Y'all would be lucky to have a bitch like me as a mother. I could teach the three of you a thing or two."

"We didn't come here to discuss our age or go back and forth. To be honest, you shouldn't even be addressing them because they're not a part of this. I'm the one that will be overseeing everything. Anything either one you have to say can be addressed to me," Promyse spoke up. For the first time since she showed that she had a little backbone. I wasn't impressed cause I would be damned if I let a couple of bitches I was in charge of disrespect me.

"Oh really?" I smiled. "I don't see how you're overseeing a damn thing when you can't talk with confidence. Your voice is shaky ma and ain't no one gon' listen to a chick that can't command respect. I don't know why Smoke would waste your time, but I don't need supervision. I'm good. You, on the other hand, need to work out your queen pin aura cause right now you ain't got it."

"Smoke isn't wasting my time. He gave me a job, and I plan on doing it. Now if you don't mind I would like to tell him we had a good lunch."

"Then I guess you should get up and have lunch with ya friends. Ain't shit good about what's going on right now. I said what I said. I'm not speaking on the shit anymore. You can dismiss ya self cause I'm not into this shit right here.

Smoke had to be smoking if he thought I was going to take orders from a thotler. It was an insult that he would even send her my way. I pulled my phone out and started texting Smoke. Boss or not Smoke was going to respect me as a woman and as a leader in his camp.

"Excuse me," the waitress said, coming over to the table. "Do you ladies know what you would like to order?"

"Me and my cousin need a little more time. However, we would appreciate it if you could escort these three to a different table. Oh and if you could bring us some bread sticks that would be great," Jiya said.

"You don't have to escort us to another table because we are just fine here," Promyse told the waitress. The waitress looked between the five of us trying to figure out what to do.

"I'll just bring enough breadsticks for the five of you until you figure out what exactly you want to do."

"You see I tried to be nice to ya ass in this fine establishment, but I see I got to show my ass to get some respect. I didn't ask you to do what you thought was best nor did I ask for breadsticks for five. I asked you to escort them to another table, and that's what I need you to do."

"I..."

"I nothing. You need to tell the three of them to get the hell up and go on about their business."

"I can't just force them to get up ma'am. The most I can do is ask them to move."

"Then what the fuck are you standing here for if all you can do is ask them to move. I can do that shit myself. Just walk away because you're 2.5 away from not getting a tip!" Jiya spat. "I was gon' give this bitch a whole five dollars. Now her ass is only getting a dollar," Jiya mumbled, and I busted out laughing. The waitress must've heard her too cause she rolled her eyes at Jiya and sucked her teeth.

"You didn't have to go in on her like that. She was just trying to do her job."

"Her job was to get those three from our table. It wasn't that hard of a job, and her slow ass couldn't do it."

"Maybe if you were nicer, she would've told them to get up."

"I guess that's something we will never know now. Who are you texting?"

"Smoke to let him know I didn't appreciate how he tried to play me."

"Make sure you let his big head ass know that I'm not feeling him on this shit either. He should've known better than to do us foul like that. I can't believe he had the line leader of the third grade show up. Like the fuck can she do besides cry and shit?"

Jiya and I busted out laughing not caring how everyone else in the restaurant was looking at us. We were carrying on with our conversation like Promyse and her toddler gang wasn't sitting across from us. The insults kept going until Lola slammed her hand on the table.

"Uh excuse you but don't go slamming your hand on the table. We're in a public place, and you need to act accordingly," I told her.

"Shut the fuck up about acting accordingly because neither of you heffas are acting like grown woman. What you mad because Smoke put a young chick in charge? I mean I guess if I were y'all too hags I would be pissed too. I would be pissed cause my boss knew that I wasn't competent enough to do my job. I would be pissed because a chick barely legal would be telling me what to do all the while never getting her hands dirty. But that's not even the part that would really piss me off. What would have me on ten is the young bitch that's my boss would be cakin' more than me just for telling me what to do.

So yeah I guess you can say I understand why the two of you are salty. But what the two of y'all are not going to do is talk about us like we're not sitting at the table. These two may not want to speak up for themselves, but my mouth is big enough to hold all three of us down. Watch your mouth and the shit that comes out of it because you got the right one," Lola sassed.

"Chill out Jiya; I know them lil' infant words ain't hurt your feelings."

She was biting her bottom lip, and that meant one thing. Jiya was ready to fuck some shit up and once she got the point that she exploded wasn't no bringing her back until she handled her business.

"You already know they didn't cause she and them words ain't shit. Matter of fact I'm not even going to take it there. I'm going to murder you with these words then spank you on the ass for disobeying ya mother."

"Bitch, my mother's a hoe so if you want to be that bitch then fine by me." Lola laughed. The other two laughed with Lola, and that was my cue to give it to their ass live and direct.

"The fuck the two of you laughing at? Neither one of you has room to laugh or even talk at this point. You allowed us to disrespect you right to your faces like y'all ain't shit. Nah, fuck that y'all ain't shit. Smoke is a fool if he thinks ya dumb ass can handle a bitch with a mouth like mine. If you can't handle my mouth how the fuck you gonna handle a bitch that likes gunplay? Your lil' ass probably couldn't handle a water gun let alone a bitch of my stature. Fuck Smoke thought trying to put my son in charge. This lil' bitch wouldn't last a day fucking with me.

That's what's wrong with these niggas. They get these young bitches with the fresh pussy and try to put them on top of the world knowing damn well they can't even handle a city. I might put it on a nigga so he knows what that good pussy feel like so he can get his mind right. Jiya what you think?"

"I'm just saying if you fuckin' Smoke I might as well give Khy all this pretty pussy. I'm not feeling the way his girl spoke to you anyway so it would only be right. She wanted to act like someone was fuckin' her man now someone will be." Jiya laughed. Her laughed was interrupted by Paulie's hand connecting with her face.

I couldn't lie her smacking Jiya caught me off guard cause I ain't think she was bout that life.

"I wish you would come at my nigga with that stank ass pussy. I may not have been saying much, but you're not about to talk about stealing my man like I won't fuck you up behind that shit."

"Did that bitch just put her hands on me?" Jiya asked me.

"Yes the fuck I did, and it was a long time coming. Popping all that shit like someone is a pun....AHHHH!"

Jiya's reached over the table and snatching Paulie up. She pulled Paulie on the table then dropped her ass on the floor. I looked at Lola and Promyse to see what they were about to do. They never looked at me. Lola went and jumped on Jiya and Promyse called herself trying to attack me and pull me out the booth. When her dumb ass reached for me, I punched her in the face then grabbed her hair. I wrapped it around my hand and was about to hit her, but I stopped myself. Instead of beating her ass I was going to use this as a teaching moment.

"I could beat your ass, but I'm not even going to do that to you. This ain't you ma, and you need to realize that now before it's too late. Smoke got you in here trying to be something that you're not. People die every day for pretending, and I know you don't want to be next. You're one of those Park Avenue princesses that got caught up in the bad boy. You're used to the finer things in life, and when a nigga from the wrong side of the tracks came along, you got excited. You thought it would be your chance to take a walk on the wild side. I'm here to tell you that the wild side ain't a place for a bitch like you to be walkin'. People get killed for less out here don't get caught up in trying to be something that you're not. Take your friends and get the fuck out of here." I let her hair go then pushed her to the floor.

Bending down, I pulled out my lil' friend from ankle strap and let two off in the air. The restaurant cleared out, but Lola, Paulie, and Jiya were still going at it. Jiya was fucking Paulie up, and Lola was hitting Jiya, but it didn't seem to be doing any damage. I snatched Lola up and rested my gun against her temple.

"Get the fuck out of here cause as much as I respect you for speaking up, that shit can go out the window along with your life." I pushed her to the side next to her friend then pulled Jiya off of Paulie. Paulie was on the floor bleeding from her mouth and nose. I shook my head cause Jiya fucked her little ass up. I pulled her up by her hair and whispered in her ear.

"I should put a bullet in your just for all that rowdy shit you was talkin' on that phone. You ain't a killer so don't make yourself out to be about that life. You don't have to worry bout no one wanting ya man cause I already had that. You should already know tho cause I'm sure you tasted my sweet pussy against his lips." I let her hair go and stood up.

Jiya looked like she wanted to charge at Lola, but I stopped her before she could even get started.

"The cops are on the way Jiya; we have to go. No one got time to be fuckin' with these minors."

"Fine!" she spat, heading towards the exit. I followed close behind her walking out like we weren't the ones that caused a scene. When we got in my car, I sped off never looking back.

"What we gon' do cause you know Smoke ain't bout to let us stay down after he hears what happened."

"It ain't Smoke that we have to give a fuck about at this point."

"Then who is it cause I could've sworn we were workin' for that nigga."

"We may be workin' for that nigga, but I can bet a hundred grand that Promyse's thoughts of us is going to hold weight on whether we keep working with Smoke or not."

"Then we fuckin' screwed." Jiya huffed.

"I don't think we are. I ain't fight Promyse for a reason. I dropped knowledge on her cause it will get further with her then my fist would. The shit I said will have her thinking, and when the time is right, she'll come to me."

"You really think she's still gonna want to fuck with you after that shit?"

"Yup."

Promyse was a young girl that I could tell needed guidance. Her eyes were literally the key to her soul. I saw everything I needed to, and I was going to use it to my advantage. I may have called her spoiled and privileged, but she was anything but. For that reason alone, I knew she would be at my door.

Chapter Nineteen

SMOKE

"I can't believe you set me up to go meet with a bitch like that. You know she had the nerve to talk shit to me when I wasn't doing anything but being nice to her? Smoke I can't do this. Ain't no way I can get her and her cousin to listen to me. I have never been scared to fight anyone or to tell anyone off, but she and her cousin had me on edge."

I listened to Promyse go on and on about how things went with Bliss and Jiya. Everything she told me I expected to happen except for the fighting. I knew Bliss and Jiya weren't going to respect Promyse because of her age and how she carried herself. I sent her there not to be successful but to learn something. I need Promyse to learn that there was always going to be someone bigger, prettier, smarter, and faster than you. That was the first lesson everyone needed to learn when getting in the game. You could change your mindset to adapt to all types of people and take from them to enhance yourself once you knew that.

I may not have wanted to admit, but I learned a lot of stuff from the old heads my father had on the team. I took the way my father and them did things and figured out ways to make it profitable for me. I may not have been down with how they did things, but when I flipped their ideas, mannerism, and business mindset, I found things that worked for me. Because of that, I'm not that nigga around town that everyone wants to be like. I need Promyse to be that bitch that every chick wanted to be like. The only way that was going to happen was if she rocked with Bliss and Jiya. More so Bliss then Jiya. Jiya was crazy as hell, and I didn't need Promyse picking up on any of that shit.

Bliss, on the other hand, was perfect. She was smart, street savvy, and sexy in a way that made everything she did easier. She was the perfect teacher for Promyse. I just needed Promyse to see that instead of letting what happened get the best of her.

"Smoke, are you listening to me?"

"I hear you talkin' ma, but I don't think it's that big of a deal."

"What do you mean it's not that big of a deal? She said I was a Park Avenue princess and you know that's the last thing that I am. She tried to make it seem that I was this privileged girl who just wanted a bad boy for the thrill of things. Like I couldn't handle being in her world or that it was too much for me."

"Is any of that true?"

"No"

"Ight then what's the point of being pissed off about something that's not true."

"I'm pissed because she was disrespectful as hell. Paulie's face is a mess because of her and her cousin. Lola even got fucked up a little bit."

"Hol' up when you started chillin' with her again?" I asked completely off guard.

"A couple of days ago I think. I don't know. She came to us apologizing, so I forgave her. That's not even what's important right now."

"That shit is important. When were you going to tell me that you started back rocking with that bitch."

"I didn't know it was something I had to tell you. You don't tell me who you're rocking with."

"That's cause everyone I rock with is an on a business level, and none of them tried to snake me the way Lola tried to snake you. You don't need to be fuckin' with that bitch. She's all out for self and you gon' fall short if you fuckin' with her."

"What's your problem with Lola? You're talking like you got a personal issue with her."

"My personal issue is that she came for you when she had no reason to. She took that one night of us fuckin' and turned it into some type of fantasy shit."

"She apologized, and I'm not going to hold it against her. I mean I was being cautious with her before, but after the way she stuck up for me today, I can't hold what she did against her."

"Fuck that. If you can't, I'll hold it against her. She doesn't deserve your friendship."

"I appreciate you being concerned but I think that's a choice I have to make on my own. This ain't even about Lola. This is about Bliss. I can't work with them, Shaheem." She sighed.

"I'm gon' tell you this once then I'm not saying it again. Can't should never be in your vocabulary. Can't means you're not capable of doing something. Promyse, you're capable of doing anything you put your mind too. You're not just some average chick that I took off the streets and said here run this trap. You're the girlfriend and future wife of the king of New York. Whatever I can do, you can do. Shit is rocky right now, but it ain't nothing for you to fix."

"Why do I have to fix it? Can't you just fix it for me?" She pouted.

"If I fix it what respect is that going to get you? In this game, you have two ways of running things. It's either your team fears you, or they respect you. I run my shit with fear, but you're nothing like me. You're not the type to the pull the trigger without blinking and walking away. I, on the other hand, could give a fuck about taking someone's life.

You have to run shit with respect, and the only way to gain someone's respect is to show them that you ain't gon' let them bully you. Bliss says you're not about that life, so you need to show her that this life is embedded in your DNA. Show her that this shit ain't nothing but a G thang to you baby. Once you do that, she'll respect ya shit, and you won't have another problem out of her."

"Why can't I just work with you or something?"

"Cause I can't handle business and have you up underneath me. I'm saying if I'm gon' be out here running shit, I need my queen out here running shit too. This a team effort I can't carry you, and you for damn sure ain't bout to carry me. We each play a part in this shit. Stop acting like you ain't that bitch."

"I mean I guess." She sighed and leaned in to kiss me.

I kissed her back assuring her that she was going to be fine. Promyse was gon' have to handle her business and stopped expecting me to come to her rescue. Don't get me wrong if shit hit the fan I would save her without a doubt, but this shit wasn't even that serious, and she wanted me to handle it. Bliss was a lot to handle, but she wasn't anything Promyse couldn't handle.

"Where's my mom?" Promyse asked, pulling away from the kiss.

"When I got here she was gone. She ain't tell you where she was going?" Panic was in her eyes, but her voice was even like she was trying to keep herself calm.

"No."

"Don't stress she probably just went out to get some food or something."

"We have food here she didn't have to leave the house."

"What did you want for her to stay locked up in here? You can't expect her to stay in the house. She needs fresh air just like the rest of us."

"Unlike the rest of us, she has an addiction. Going outside could undo all the progress she made in rehab."

"It's not going to happen like that."

"You don't know that."

"I don't but what I do know is if you keep her on a short leash you're going to drive her right back to doing drugs. You have to let her breath."

"I'm not letting her breath. I just got the mother that I've always wanted. I'm not going to let her breath so that she can go back to her old self. I refuse to deal with that again. I just want her to stay clean."

"She will stay clean as long as you don't watch her every move. You need to have a one on one conversation with her and let her know how you're feeling."

"What good will that do?"

"It will create an honest relationship between the two of you. Right now y'all are acting like everything is fine instead of being honest with each other. You need to tell your moms how much she hurt you, so y'all can move on."

"I don't think that's the right thing to do right no..." Her words were cut off by the ringing of my phone.

I looked at the screen and saw Saigon's name flashing across the screen.

"Hol up I need to take this," I told Promyse.

"Don't worry about it I'm about to go for a walk."

"You ight?" I asked her before answering the phone. I knew the topic of her mother was a heavy one, but I ain't think she was going to get emotional behind it.

"Yeah I'm fine, I just need some air."

"Ight, if you need me come back this way."

"Okay." She kissed me on the cheek then left out.

I watched her walk out while dialing Saigon back. It was true what Lil Wayne said. I hated to see her go but loved to watch her leave. Promyse ain't know it yet, but she was gon' be the biggest thing to come out of Marcy Projects.

Chapter Twenty

PAULIE

"What the fuck happened to your face?" Khy barked when I walked in the door.

Instead of answering him, I rolled my eyes and sucked my teeth. I had no room to be upset with Khy, but I was livid. I didn't know for sure if he slept with Bliss, but I knew if he did he slept with her before me. What was before me was simple before me and didn't matter right now. What had me pissed was a bitch thinking it was that simple to just sleep with my man. The way Jiya was so comfortable saying how she was going to sleep with Khy didn't sit right with me. Add that to the fact that she beat my ass, and the result was Khy getting all this attitude.

"Paulina, stop playing with me and tell me what happened to your face?" he barked, getting off the couch and following me into the bedroom.

"I'm walking away because I don't want to throw this misdirected anger your way, but if you keep pressing me I'ma go off," I warned.

"Fuck all that. What happened to your face and I'm not gonna ask you again?"

I laughed because he just didn't know when to leave well enough alone.

"Your bitch is what happened to my face."

"You did that to ya self?" he asked stupidly.

"No dumbass, your bitch beat my ass."

"Yo watch ya mouth smart ass. I ain't got no bitch but you."

"Not according to Jiya. If you let her tell it, she can fuck you off GP. I thought she was out of line when she said that, so I slapped her. Me slapping her resulted on me getting my ass beat!" I spat. I started stripping out of my clothes because all I wanted to do was soak my body in a nice hot bath.

"When were you with Jiya?"

"It doesn't matter when what matters is can she sleep with you if she wanted too?"

"Hell no, she can't. You shouldn't even have to ask me that shit cause you know what it is."

"No, I thought I knew what it was, but I was obviously wrong. But guess what else I found out?"

Khy ain't say nothing. He just glared at me like he wanted to beat my ass. I didn't understand what he was upset about when I was the one with the fucked up face.

"Since you don't want to guess I'll tell. I found out that not only can Jiya fuck you when she wants to but that you fucked Bliss."

"Fuck you hear that shit? I ain't fuck Bliss?"

"You sure cause she seemed sure that you had her pussy all in your mouth. She tried to say that she fucked you while you were with me, but I know better. I know better because you know better than to sleep with another chick while you're with me."

"I'm not bout to do this shit with you, Paulie."

"Why not? You got something you want to tell me?"

"I don't got shit to tell, and that's why I'm not doing this shit with you."

"Mhmm. Now I'm starting to think you fucked her while you were with me."

"Think what the fuck you want," he said, waving me off.

"No, you tell me what the fuck to think, Khyree! Did you or did you not sleep with her while you were with me?"

"Man, kill that shit and get dressed."

"I'm not getting dressed, and you're not leaving this house! Did you fuck the bitch or not? I swear to God if you fucked her Khy, I'm killing you and then I'ma kill that bitch."

"You ain't gon do shit. Shut ya punk ass up and get dressed."

"Oh nigga, you think this is a game? Don't let my young age fool you!" I gritted.

I went and stormed out the room and headed straight for the kitchen. I grabbed the sharpest knife I could find and headed back to the bedroom. If I knew where Khy kept his guns, I would've grabbed one of those. Since Khy wanted to play like I wasn't about that life I was going to show him just how much I was. I got played by them bitches at the restaurant, and I wasn't about to be played by my man.

"Pauline put the fucking knife down and get dressed!" Khy demanded when I walked back in the room.

"Nigga, fuck you!" I yelled and charged him. He stood up from the bed and tripped my ass. I fell face first on the floor.

"Khy, ya lucky I didn't stab myself because of that shit!" I yelled and jumped up. I left the knife on the floor cause I didn't need to fuck up and hurt myself.

"You wasn't gonna stab ya self. Get dressed," he told me again.

"Fuck you Khyree! I'm not doing shit but getting my ass in the tub. Dumb ole cheating ass muthafucka!" I spat. I went to walk out the room when this crazy muthafucker snatched my ass up. He yanked me back then placed his hand at my throat.

"Khy, get the fuck off me!" I yelled.

I played it like I wasn't scared, but on the inside, I was scared shitless. I wasn't saying that Khy was like his father, but he could've been just like his father. Abuse was learned, and if watched his mother go through all that abuse with his father there was no telling what his crazy ass picked up.

"When I tell you to do somethin' Paulie you fuckin' do it. If you would've got fuckin' dressed you would've got the answer to your fuckin' question. Instead, you wanna run ya mouth and do dumb shit like grabbing knives knowing damn well you ain't gon' do shit with it. Get the fuck dressed now and meet me outside. You got ten minutes." He let me go, and I stumbled a little.

"I'm not your child and you can't talk to me like I'm one. And don't you ever in ya life put your fuckin' hands on me. I'm not your mother and you're not your father!" I yelled.

"You right cause I wouldn't kill you like my punk ass daddy did. I would just leave ya ass the fuck alone and act like you never existed. Get dressed!"

I watched him walk out the room and tears started to fall from my eyes. Him yoking me up no longer mattered neither did if he slept with Bliss while we were together. What mattered was him being able to walk away from me and act like I didn't exist. I walked over to the mirror and looked at myself. The person I that was looking back at me was someone I didn't recognize. This wasn't the strong head Paulie. I ain't know who the fuck this girl was, but I refused to become her anymore.

All the fighting Khy and I were doing was going to stop today. I was tired of it and if we didn't fix it then there wouldn't be an us. I refused to believe that Khy would be able to just walk away from me like I wasn't the best thing to happen to him. I wiped the tears from my face and got myself together. Crying wasn't going to fix anything. The only way this was going to work was if Khy and I got our shit together. I said Khy and I because this wasn't just on me. He allowed himself to get to the point he wrapped his hand around my neck, and I wasn't going for that.

I hurried and got dressed then washed my face in the bathroom. I didn't plan on going anywhere with Khy, I just wanted to talk about what happened and how it wasn't going to happen again. When I got outside, I went right over to the car and knocked on his window.

"Get in the car Paulie." He sighed.

"Get out the car. We need to discuss a few things."

"We can discuss them in the car just get in."

"No! I need to make sure I have room to run just in case ya crazy ass tries to choke me again."

Khy looked at me then got out the car. He leaned up against his door and stared at me before talking. "That's really what you think we've come to? We at the point you think I would put my hands on you in a way to hurt you."

"From what you did back there ain't no telling what you're capable of."

"Ight, say no more."

He went to get back in the car and I stopped him. "Running away from our problems isn't going to fix anything. We need to talk this out cause the next time you put your hands on me I'm leaving you."

"And you pulling a knife on a nigga is okay?"

"I'm not saying that's okay, but what I'm saying is we were both wrong. We let our emotions get the best of us. Neither one of us liked where it went, so we need to talk about not letting it happen again."

"Paulie, I'm not the person my father was. I fucked up by yoking you up, but you wouldn't fuckin' listen. You wanted to keep questioning me about a bitch that you don't even know. The when I tell you to get dressed so we can handle the situation, you wanna resist and talk shit. I don't got time to be going through the bullshit with you Paulie. I'm trying to be the best nigga I can be for you, but shit's gotta change. I've been saying this for the longest, but I mean it now. We both need to get our anger in check, or we need to go about our business."

"I'll fix my attitude, but you can't tell me I didn't have every right to go off the way I did."

"You didn't cause there was no truth behind any of that shit you was throwing my way. I ain't fuck Bliss, and I damn sure don't plan on fuckin' Jiya."

"You could've just said that and the problem would've been solved."

"Shit don't get solved by me just telling you that. In the back of your mind, the thought would've still been there. The only way to dead the shit is to bring you face to face with ole girl. That way shit can be put to rest the way it needs to be. Now let's go."

"Okay," I told him then got in the car.

I didn't know how this was going to play out going to see Jiya and Bliss. I mean I wasn't scared or nothing, but I damn sure wasn't ready to see her again. I wanted to be able to handle my battles on my own. I didn't want Khy always coming to my rescue. If things went left then I would put Jiya in her place, I would just have to be ready to potentially get my ass beat once again.

Chapter Twenty-One

KHYREE

The shit that went down with Paulie had me fucked up in the head. She made a nigga show a side of me that I wasn't trying to show. It seemed like whenever we argued she had my head fucked up, but this time I took shit too far. I'm not gon' lie it took a lot out of me to not squeeze her neck as tight as I could. All I was trying to do was put shit to rest, and she wanted to wild out. I've said it before and I was going to say it again, shit had to change.

On the way to Jiya's crib, shit was on mute. Paulie wasn't saying shit and neither was I. The only person I had conversation for was Jiya, Bliss, and that nigga Smoke. Jiya and Bliss was gettin' it off the fact Paulie's face was fucked up. I was shocked as fuck that Jiya fucked her up that bad. With all the mouth Paulie has, I thought she could handle herself. I was gon' have to put her ass in boxing or something cause she couldn't be going around talkin' shit and gettin' beat up. Smoke was gon' hear my mouth cause this shit was his fault.

He put Promyse in charge of two bitches that he knew she couldn't handle. Promyse wasn't the take charge type and because of that she would bring Paulie into this shit. As long as I was around, Paulie wasn't fucking with shit that had to do with this game. If Promyse couldn't handle the bullshit then that was on her. She would have to find the courage to tell Smoke she ain't want this shit. I would be damn if I let her drag Paulie into this shit. Don't get it fucked up, Promyse was like the baby sis but Paulie's well-being came first and always would. Smoke was dumb as fuck for bringing Promyse in, but you couldn't tell that nigga shit cause he swore he knew everything.

I pulled up to Jiya's crib and texted her telling her to come outside. She wasted no time walking out of her building and walking up to my car.

"Damn, don't tell me you went home and told ya nigga on me. I thought you were going to take that ass-whoopin' like the woman you're trying to be," was the first thing out of Jiya's mouth when Paulie and I stepped out the car.

I went to say something but Paulie stopped me.

"Bitch, I ain't tell my nigga shit. He was concerned about what happened to my face as he should be."

"Mhm, I guess. Khy, what did you tell me to come outside for?"

"See this is what we're not going to do. When I'm talking to you, you listen. Don't question my man when you're a bitch just like I'm one," Paulie told her.

"Oh look who found her voice. I guess ya man over here put a battery in ya back. Don't let that gas you cause I'll fuck you up in front of ya nigga and then suck his dick."

"Jiya, watch that shit!" I started to say because she was getting disrespectful as fuck.

"No Khy, I got this. Bitch, if you want to suck his dick then be my guess. I'll pull his jeans down and hold it for you if you want. But, know if you suck his dick then you licking my pussy. My nigga is the one running the show. My nigga is the one that gave you your job. My nigga is the reason why you're able to feed ya self in live in this bum ass apartment complex. Since my nigga is the one that made it possible to do all of that, that makes me responsible for you still breathing. As easily as my man gave you all this shit, I can be the one to take it away. So yeah, you may have had me shook earlier, and you even beat my ass, but the one thing you can't do is take anything away from me the way I can take it away from you. So if you want to please my nigga, then you gon' please me too boo cause we one in the same."

Paulie talking that shit had my shit on brick. It was bout time she realized who she was fuckin' with, and the type of clout that she got for fuckin' with a nigga like me. See Smoke was trying to toughen Promyse up by throwing her to the wolves. I, on the other hand, didn't have to do the shit cause Paulie was one that could figure the shit out for herself. Once she fell, she was sure to get back up with a vengeance."

"Bitch, I wish I would lick ya shit. You talkin' all that shit about what you can take from me, but that ain't shit. Everything he takes I can get back and double the shit. I'm not fuckin' for mine I'm workin' for it. And just like this nigga got work, so does any other nigga," Jiya sassed.

I shook my head cause she was worse than Bliss. Bliss gave in when I told her how shit was gon' play. Jiya wanted to continue the tough act like she didn't need this shit.

"That's what's wrong with you. Instead of just bowing out gracefully, you wanna continue the tough shit. You can do what the fuck you want. If you want to get down with another team, then go do that. My nigga and his team don't need no one that can't humble themselves. Just make sure you let Bliss know shit was your fault when you tell her that y'all ain't down no more. Come on Khy; I'm ready to go home."

I leaned over grabbed my baby in my arms and tongued her down. I was proud of her for standing up to Jiya. She let it be known that she ain't need her nigga to handle shit for her cause she could hold it down on her own.

"I respect it," Jiya said, interrupting our kiss. "My bad for the shit I was talkin' earlier. You proved yourself."

"Shawty ain't got to prove herself to no one," I told Jiya.

"Cut the shit Khy cause you know damn well she's gon' have to prove herself to every person she comes in contact with. Let me tell you something Paulie, being with a nigga that is at the top of this drug shit ain't easy. Every person that Khy introduces you to is gon' try you on some level. They're going to try you to make sure that you're the right one to be sitting next to Khy at the top. Like you said you're a reflection of ya man and that means you have to be as strong as he is. That nigga wouldn't let no one punk him, and you can't let no one punk you. You have to carry yourself as if you're the baddest bitch in the game cause if you don't the next bitch that does think she's the baddest will be first in line to take ya spot."

"I hear you," was all Paulie said to that. To my surprise, Jiya reached out and hugged Paulie.

"My bad about ya face."

"Don't worry about cause payback is a bitch," Paulie told her.

"What you trying to say?"

"It's on sight for ya ass. Don't think because we got an understanding shit is cool. I owe you one," Paulie told her.

"Shit, pick a time and a place. I'm foreva ready." Jiya laughed.

"Ight," Paulie said then slipped back in the car.

I got in behind her then drove off trying to figure out what the fuck happened. I ain't never seen two girls make up the way Jiya and Paulie did. I wasn't even gon' question that shit or speak on it. Things were cool, and that was all I cared about.

$ $ $

"What happened last night? I was tryin' to call you. Saigon and Fame hit me. They wanted us to come thru Jersey," Smoke said.

"I was busy handling shit with Paulie and Jiya. Jiya fucked Paulie up at the meeting Promyse was at."

"The fuck was Paulie doing at the meeting?" Smoke asked, playing dumb.

"Nigga, you know damn well that Promyse wasn't going to roll to that meeting dolo. Wherever Promyse goes, Paulie's down to ride ass ain't too far behind."

"Damn, that's crazy. I ain't think shit was gon' to go left like that. Bliss and Jiya are rowdy, but I ain't think they were that rowdy."

"How could you not know? Bliss and Jiya are both the type of bitches that don't give a fuck about nothing another bitch has to say. Promyse is the type to play the background. She's not built for this shit. You need to pull her out."

"I'm not pulling her out of shit. She can handle this cause she's my girl. Worry bout ya chick getting beat up and shit."

"The fuck you say?" I barked. Smoke had me fucked up. He was trying me a lot lately, and I wasn't with it. "I'm not one of your flunkies or the niggas that work for you. You're not gonna keep saying slick shit and expect me not to do shit bout it."

"I'm just saying, don't worry about a bitch you ain't fuckin'. I know what's best for Promyse. She can handle things out in Harlem."

"How can she handle Harlem when Bliss damn near walked over her ass?"

"Bliss is gon' toughen Promyse up. Sooner or later Promyse is going to bounce back on her ass. Stop worrying I got this. I wouldn't let Promyse do nothing that would get her hurt.

"Yeah ight, nigga. Just watch the shit you be talkin'. I don't disrespect Promyse so don't disrespect Paulie. You're my brother and all, but I'll fuck a nigga up behind that one."

"Say less," Smoke said, dapping me up.

"What them niggas want us out in Jersey for? They just left from here not too long ago."

"They havin' a party out there to welcome us to the team."

"When is it?"

"Tonight."

"I can't do it. Paulie wants to spend time together. Shit's been crazy with us, and I'm tryin' to just kick it with her on some relax shit."

"Y'all can kick it at the party. It's gon' be crazy. From what I hear them niggas do it up. And shit gon' look all bad if the guest of honor doesn't roll through. If anything, bring Paulie with you. Promyse is coming with me."

"How I'ma bring her to the party when her face is fucked up?"

"Tell her to throw some makeup on that shit. Nigga this gon' be a party to remember and you telling me you not about to come through because ya girl face is fucked up and she wants to chill?"

"Paulie comes before all this shit. If she ain't down, then a nigga ain't down."

"My nigga, you pussy whipped. Damn, I ain't think you were gonna go out like that." Smoke laughed.

"Who said I was whipped? I'm tryin' to do right by my girl, and that's it. I ain't chase her to just walk all over her. What we have is deep and no matter how much we argue that's my baby right there. Money doesn't give me the same feeling I get when I'm around Paulie. Paulie makes ya boy feel like he a king or some shit. Shawty will always come first in my eyes."

"I don't need my chick to make me feel like a king cause a nigga know he a king. I ain't knockin' you for how you feel tho. That shit was deep. Just see if she wants to slide through."

"Ight."

"What you want to do bout Jiya and Bliss. I know you're not feeling them putting hands on Paulie."

"I handle it already. I took Paulie when I went to deal with Jiya last night."

"You handled Jiya? Say word?"

"I went to handle Jiya, but Paulie stepped in and handled her business."

"Shit, Paulie stepping up and handling business. I might have to get her down with the team."

"She ain't fuckin' with this shit. You want Promyse to be trappin' cool, but Paulie ain't on that."

"I was jokin' chill, my nigga." Smoke laughed, but that shit wasn't funny to me.

"I'm just sayin' Paulie ain't with that shit."

"I heard you the first time. Since you took care of Jiya, I'll handle Bliss. She needs to understand not to step out of place."

"Ight. I'm up," I told him.

I dapped Smoke up then headed back to the crib to see if Paulie was down to go to his party. I already knew she wasn't gonna want to go. She wasn't tryin' to let me out her sight today. The only reason I was able to link up with Smoke was cause her ass fell asleep. She was 'posed to be putting ya boy to sleep, but I had to switch shit up on her ass.

I was cool with not going to the party cause I wasn't feeling that nigga Fame. Saigon was cool cause he kept shit short and to the point. Fame was moving like he ain't trust Smoke and me, or he had something against us. I ain't know about that nigga, but I wasn't in the business of keepin' company around I didn't trust. That nigga was a different breed, and I wasn't trying to be around it. All I needed was for our business to be straight and I was good. Anything personal I ain't want any parts of. If Paulie was down to go to the party, then I wasn't gon' have a choice but to go. Not showing face would've been bad for business.

I jumped in my whip ready to pull off when Mercy call came through on my phone. I sent her first call to voicemail, but then she kept ringing my phone down.

After a while, I got tired of hearing my phone ringing and answered her call.

"Yo!' I answered.

"Hey, why you duckin' my calls? I thought we were good."

"We were good, but I can't have you ringing my shit down like that, Mercy. I told you what it was already."

"I know you have a girl and that has nothing to do with me or why I'm calling. I just wanted to see if you were coming to the party Saigon and Fame are throwing."

"I mean the shit is for Smoke and I. It would be rude for me not to show face."

"True, but I just wanted to make sure that you were gonna come. You know how you can be." She giggled. I ain't know what the fuck she was talking about cause she didn't even know how I could be.

"Ight if that's all you called for I gotta go."

"Wait, don't hang up!"

"What is it, Mercy?"

"I just wanted to remind you that I don't mind being number two. You can always call me when your girl fucks up or when she's not ridin' it right. I know how you like it daddy and I know just how tight to squeeze. Say the word, and I'll rock ya world, and ya girl will never know."

"Mercy I..."

"Save it cause I don't even need an answer right now. Just think on it," she cooed then hung up the phone.

I ran my hand over my face cause this was the shit I didn't need. Telling Paulie was startin' to look like the right move. She might surprise me and forgive a nigga for what he did. I was lying to myself cause wasn't no way in hell she was gon' rock with a nigga after what I did. I was gon' have to take this secret to the grave cause Paulie was gon' be by my side for a lifetime and then some.

Chapter Twenty-Two

LOLA

"Dr. Johnson I would appreciate if you would stop calling my phone. You already gave me my death sentence what more do we have to talk about?" I questioned.

I was tired of him calling my phone damn near every two hours. I started to put his number on my block list, but I knew I was gonna have to see him. I was just trying to hold off on seeing him until I got Smoke to come with me. There was no point in dealing with it alone when I had a lover who was going through the same thing.

"I'm calling you because I need you to come down to my office. We have a few things that we need to discuss."

"We have nothing to discuss. I'm not ready to deal with the fact I have HIV. You will know when I'm ready to deal with it and start getting treatment. Until then just let me live my life and be at peace," I huffed.

"I'm not supposed to speak of this over the phone, but it's something you have to know. I don't need you doing anything hasty, and then it being on my conscious. I'm going to bend the rules, but once I do, you need to get down to my office." He paused for a second I guess to see if I was going to agree. I wasn't agreeing to anything until I found out what he had to say.

"Your positive test result was a false positive."

"What you mean a false positive?" I asked shocked.

"Sometimes when the rapid test is done patients may get a false positive. For this reason, we always run a regular blood test. As you know, those test results usually take a couple of weeks to come in. I've had your results for about two weeks which was why I kept calling you."

"Dr. Johnson, don't play with me are you serious?' I asked. I needed him to say I didn't have HIV one last time.

"I'm serious. In fact, come to my office before we close, and we can go over the standard test results."

"I'll be there within the next two hours. Thank you so much, Dr. Johnson. I'm gon' suck the skin off your dick because of this," I beamed then hung up the phone.

I jumped off my bed and started twerking. There was no music playing, but a bitch was twerking to the words Dr. Johnson just spoke to me. Today was literally the second best day of my life. The first was Smoke and me fucking. I mean this was close to being first, but nothing topped the way Smoke's dick felt when it was deep inside of me.

"Oh shit, I have to call Smoke!" I said aloud.

I quickly dialed his number and waited for him to answer. His phone rang out and went to voicemail. I called again, and the same thing happened. I called at least ten more times and got the same results. I thought about leaving a message, but this wasn't something I wanted to tell him over the phone. He deserved to get this message in person. I thought us having HIV together would bring us closer together. Boy was I wrong because his ass was keeping his distance. I was kind of glad though because waiting it out showed me that the big guy above had a better way to get us together.

Now that neither one of us had the package we could live happily ever after. Nothing was stopping us from being together, expect Promyse. I was going to use me having HIV as a way to get her out. Now that I knew I was clean my plan was gonna have to change. I had to come up with something epic because Smoke and Promyse were closer than I thought. This nigga bought that bitch a car. Not just any car but MY fuckin' dream car. What kind of bullshit was that? What made it worse was the fact she couldn't drive. Her car and man should've been mine, but in due time they were going to be. I needed to find some dirt on Promyse. It was no longer about turning Promyse off from Smoke. I had to turn Smoke off from Promyse.

$ $ $

"So, are we going to the party tonight or what?" I heard Promyse ask as I walked into the living room.

"What party and put Paulie on speaker so I can hear the convo," I told her.

"I'm not going to no party. My face is all fucked up, and I refuse to go into public looking like this," Paulie complained.

"Put some makeup on your face Paulie and let's go have fun. We haven't been to one party this whole summer. We start school soon, and I just want to end summer with a bang."

"I'm gonna ask this again cause you bitches ain't paying me any mind. What party?"

"A couple of Smoke's friends are throwing him a party out in Jersey. Smoke told me I'm going with him, and I want Paulie to go, so I'm not left alone."

"Am I invited to this party?" I questioned.

"You damn sure are. You can take Lola. Problem solved, and now I don't have to go."

"Paulie stop it because you're going."

"Damn, am I not good enough to go with?" I asked, faking hurt.

"Shut up Lola cause it's not like that. I just want the three of us to go out together."

"I don't know Promyse; I have to think about it. I don't even know how to do makeup to let alone use it to cover up bruises."

"Don't worry I got you. Just meet up with us, and I'll bring all my stuff," I told her.

"See now you have no reason not to go."

"Yeah, whatever. My man is coming through the door so I'ma talk to you bitches later."

"You mean you'll see us later." Promyse laughed.

"Yeah, that." Paulie laughed too then hung up.

"I can't wait to go out to this party tonight. I just need some fun in my life," Promyse said sitting her phone down.

"Yeah me too. Where's your mom?" I asked, changing the subject.

After leaving Dr. Johnson's office, I came over to Promyse's place. I tried to break the good doctor off with some of this good head, but he wasn't fucking with me like that. It was a waste too. I got to catch a feel, and he was working with a big something something.

"What made you bring up my mother?"

"Nothing. I just expected to see her, and I wanted to know if she was here so I could speak. You know parents think it's rude as hell when you walk into their house without speaking.

"True. She's out."

"Where did she go? You're not scared for her to be out on her own?"

"Why would I be scared?"

"Cause she might end up on drugs or something. I'm not even trying to funny I'm being serious right now. I know how it messed you up before when she was on drugs. It can only get worse if she got clean then messed up. I don't want you going through any more pain."

"I appreciate that, but I trust my mother knows what she's doing. She's grown, and I can't babysit her forever. At some point, I have to trust that she will want to do better for herself. Not for me but for herself."

"I hear that I'm just saying don't be so willing to forgive her. These things take time to get back into."

"How would you know your mom's a hoe, not an addict?" Promyse sassed.

"What you think a hoe isn't an addict? She's out here fucking and sucking niggas because she's addicted. The same way your mom put drugs before you, my mother put dick before me. I understand the pain of wanting a mother, a real one. I get it, and if my mother ever tried to come back in my life saying she was changed, I would take things slow. I'm just saying take things a day at a time and watch her."

"Do you watch your mother when she's out here slobbing on every knob she comes in contact with?"

"Ouch, that hurt." I laughed. "Wassup Promyse that was out of line."

"And what you just said to me wasn't?"

"No it wasn't, I was being a good friend and giving you advice. You're taking everything I say and trying to twist it like I'm coming at you and I'm not."

"It's your fault I'm trying to twist everything you're saying. You always have some slick shit to say, or you say things with double meanings."

"I understand that but now isn't one of them times. You're being overly sensitive."

"I'm not being overly sensitive. It just seems like lately you have an issue with me. I thought we squashed everything, but you still say sideways shit."

"No one is throwing jabs. Let that shit go, Promyse. I'm happy for you and Smoke I really am. If we're going to be friends you truly have to let what I said about the two of you go. Let it go and let us move on and stop thinking everything I say is a jab. I was bluntly honest before that's not going to change just because you got a boyfriend."

"It's hard to let something go when you can't see a person's true intentions."

"If you can't see my true intentions then we don't need to be friends. Don't you think if I were on some snake shit I would've let them girls talk to you however they wanted to? I stuck up for you at the restaurant, yet you don't know my intentions." I faked like I was hurt to gain Promyse's sympathy.

"I get that Lola, I do. Look, if you're willing to leave the past in the past then so am I. From here on out anything you said before today will stay in the past. We'll start clean, and all is forgiven."

"I don't know if I want to be your friend now."

"Shut up cause you know if you're not my friend the only friend you're gonna have is Paulie."

"I'm fine with just having Paulie."

"Yeah okay. You know you love me so stop acting like you don't.

"Whatever don't hype yoursel..."

Promyse's mom walking in the door caused my words to trail off. Her eyes were bloodshot red, and her face was flustered. There were a couple of things I wanted to say, but I bit my tongue. I had to remind myself that Promyse and I were starting over. I wasn't going to say anything right now, but best believe I was saving a couple of comments in my vault for the next time we got into it.

"Ma, what's wrong? Why are you looking like that?" Promyse asked. Secret ignored her and walked right past us.

"This seems like a private matter, so I'm going to leave. Just hit me when you want me to come back over for the party."

"Okay."

Promyse didn't bother walking me to the door. We both got up, and she headed in the direction of her mother's room, and I went for the door. My nosey ass wanted to stay and find out what was going on so bad. I had other things I needed to do so my nosiness was gonna have to be put on the back burner. I would get the story later. In the meantime, I had to find the sexiest outfit I had because I needed to look irresistible tonight. Smoke was going to notice me tonight, and when he did, I was going to make sure I sucked the skin off his dick. The good doctor didn't want this good head, so zaddy Smoke was gonna get all this mouth. That's right I was on a dick sucking mission tonight.

Chapter Twenty-Three

PROMYSE

"Ma, why did you walk right past me like I didn't say anything to you?"

"Promyse, go on. I'm not in the mood to talk right now," she told me. She couldn't even bring herself to look at me. That told me everything I needed to know. She was out doing shit she didn't need to be doing.

"Why because you went out there and got high? I can't believe I thought you changed. The first chance you got you fell right back into your old ways. I guess I don't matter to you cause you couldn't even stay clean."

"You do matter!" my mother yelled.

"How do I matter when you're walking into the house high? You don't give a fuck about me. Your addiction is so strong that you would fuckin' disappointment and crush my world. You ain't just did that shit once but you did it twice, and the second time stings the most."

Secret looked at me as I poured my heart out to her. I felt stupid as hell to think my mother would change her ways let alone be the mother I needed her to be.

"I don't even want to hear anything you have to say. Just get out! Get the fuck out my house! You won't be living here and getting high. Go out in the world and be with your favorite girl because I'm not her. It kills me to say this but it's the truth, and the truth is the only thing I have left to speak to you. I swear to God I hope the same high you chase kills you because in my eyes you're already dead."

I looked at my mother one last time and went to walk out her bedroom. Something I said must've hurt her feelings cause she got up and rushed passed me to block the doorway.

"You're not going anywhere until you listen to what I have to say," she demanded.

"I'm not listening to shit you have to say. Your words don't mean shit to me."

"Promyse, when I tell you something you listen!" my mother demanded.

"Yeah the fuck right!" I laughed. My laughed was cut short when my mother slapped the shit out of me. I went to slap her back, but she caught my wrist. I was in shock, and I'm sure it read on my face.

"Don't ever in your fucking life talk to me the way you just did. Raise your hand to me again, and I promise you I'll break your fingers. I'm not the high Secret that you've become accustomed to. I'm clean, and I refuse to tolerate disrespect from the child I brought into this world. As easily as you came is as easy as you can go. You're going to listen to what I have to say. Go sit ya ass on the bed and don't say a word until I'm done talking." She let my hand go, but I didn't move. "Promyse, don't make me tell you again. Sit ya ass the fuck down!" she yelled.

Her voice echoed against the walls scaring me a little. I took a seat on the bed and crossed my arms under my breasts.

"You have all that mouth, and only the Lord knows where you got it from because it didn't come from me. I'm not going to tolerate what I used to put up with when it came to you. I'm your mother, and you will show me the respect I deserve. Talking about you hope the high I chase is the same high that kills me cause I'm already dead to you. How can you say that when I just went through the hardest thing, I ever had to deal with for you?"

"Am I supposed to be grateful that you got clean for me because I'm not. You should've got clean for me when I asked you to. You should've got clean for me before you asked me to sell my ass. Instead, you decided to get clean for me when my boyfriend told you that you ain't have no choice but to get clean. You say how could I wish death on you like it's hard. Wishing death on you became easy once you told me that you would be my pimp. You were going to pimp me out for you fuckin' addiction, ma! How the fuck is that okay but me wishing death on you isn't" I questioned. She wasn't about to try and guilt trip me when I haven't done anything wrong.

"I know I said some things that hurt you, and I'm sorry. I'm trying to do the right thing now Promyse, but you have to let me and trust me. I'm trying to be the mother you deserve and that you want me to be. It's not going to be easy, but I'm trying. You just have to let me be that and not accuse me of doing drugs.

"How are you trying to be anything when you've been out of this house for the past two days without saying anything to anyone? You don't have friends so where are you going, ma? I'll tell you where you're going; you're out there getting high. The sad part is you don't respect me enough to tell me the truth. I'm not stupid. Your eyes are red and glossy. Your face is flushed ma! I've seen you high more times than I would've liked to, so I know what those signs mean. If you'd rather get high then to be a mother that's on you. I'm not going to stop you, but you're not going to do it here."

Tears were steady falling down my eyes, and I quickly wiped them away because I didn't want my mother seeing me crying. She didn't deserve the tears that were falling from my eyes.

"Promyse, what are you talking about? Last I check, I was grown. I'm not in rehab or jail so I can come and go as I please. I'm not out here doing drugs. I'm not getting high and don't plan to no time soon. Why are you thinking the worse of me? Did I mess you up that bad?"

"YES MA, YOU DID MESS ME UP THAT BAD! All I know is the high version of you. When I think about you, I automatically associate you with drugs. When you walk out this house without saying anything what do you want me to think? You don't have any friends to hang with, so where are you going?"

"I was walking around crying my eyes out. Being in this house with you hurts me to my soul. It kills me to be here with you because I don't deserve to be in your life. I don't deserve a second chance because I royally fucked up the first chance. It kills me that you had to find happiness with a dude who sells the very thing that stopped me from being a mother to you. I'm beyond sorry for everything I've done to you Promyse. There are not enough words in the English vocabulary to explain how sorry I am. I should've been a better mother to you, but I didn't know how to be a mother and get high. I had to make a choice, and it's sad to say, but I chose the drugs. This time around, I'm not choosing the drugs. I'm choosing you and only you, Promyse."

"That's the thing I don't need you to choose me. I need you to choose yourself." I need you to live a better life for you. I don't need a mother at this point in my life. I've grown up a long time ago and stopped looking for you to help me out. The drug dealer that makes me happy is the reason you're clean. He's the reason you have a house to come back home to. On top of that, he's the reason for my happiness, which should make you more than happy. You see I don't need anything from you. Everything that you need to do needs to be done for yourself. You have to get right with yourself before you can get right with anyone else. You have to forgive yourself for the things you've done before I forgive you. I've learned to live without a mother for so long that it's become second nature to me. Put yourself first, and then you can worry about me."

I got up from the bed and headed to the door because I couldn't do this. There was so much I wanted to say to her, but I couldn't pile it on her right now. If I did, there was a chance she would relapse. I would rather hold in my hurt then have my pain destroy her.

"Promyse just promise that in time we will have that conversation."

"What conversation?"

"The one that you're holding in. I understand why you don't want to have it now, but we need to have it at some point."

"Focus on yourself first, and then we can have that conversation. I promise."

I left out my mother's room and rushed to my own. I climbed into my bed and crawled up into a ball. I cried until I couldn't cry anymore. Something had to change because I couldn't keep doing this. When things got rough, I cried or fell into the background. I did it with Bliss, and now I was doing it with my mother. I needed to face all of my issues head on and not think twice. I couldn't be the girl that everyone felt sorry for. I needed to be the girl that everyone respected. I needed to be proud of myself instead of feeling sorry for myself, and that was going to start tonight.

Chapter Twenty-Four

SAIGON

Man I been did that, man I been popped off. And if she ain't trying to give it up he get dropped off. Let me bust that U-ie, bitch bust that open. Might spend a couple thou just to bust that open. Rip it off no joking, like your name Hulk Hogan. Niggas move weight in the south but live in Hoboken. Bitch, I spit that crack, like I'm in that trap. So if you need a hit, then I 'm with that bat.

Moving through the club, I bobbed my head to a Nicki joint the DJ was spinning. The club was thick as fuck. Anyone that was someone came out to show love to Khyree and Smoke. I appreciated everyone coming out, but I was on the lookout for one person and one person only. I made my way over to the VIP section where Fame, Smoke, Khyree, and niggas from the squad were turnin' shit the fuck out. Bottles were in hands, blunts in rotation, and each of them niggas had a bad bitch or two by their side. Smoke had to be out of it cause the chick he had by his side wasn't the female that should've been by his side.

The nigga was living foul from what I could see. He ain't have no respect for shawty, but it was cool cause I would respect her enough for the both of us. I scanned the section to see if saw who I was looking for. She was nowhere in sight which meant I didn't need to be here. I turned to head out when I felt someone bump into my chest.

"Damn nigga, watch where the fuck you going?" the girl spat, getting off the floor. Shawty had to be on the verge of being drunk cause ain't no way her ass just fell to the ground that easy.

"Chill off on the drinks and shit."

"It's an open bar so I'ma drink until I can't drink no more," she sassed, trying to wipe her dress off.

"Just cause shit is free don't mean you gotta get pissy. You're a lady ma act like one," I told her then sidestepped her.

"Muthafucker, what did you say?" she spat, grabbing my arm.

"Shawty get ya hands off me cause I don't play like that."

"Who said I'm playing? You need to apologize for what you just said to me."

"Ma, I'm telling you now let a nigga breath cause this ain't what you want," I threw over my shoulder ready to leave.

I ain't know who this bitch was, but she was gon' get some act right fuckin' with me. I never moved solo. Even when it looked like I was alone, I had a couple of bitches and niggas in the cut that ain't mind getting their hands dirty.

"No this ain't what you want!" she yelled.

I laughed and kept it pushing cause I ain't have time to play games with a bitch that couldn't handle her liquor. I was damn near out the VIP section when I felt a sharp pain in my balls. The shit hurt like fuck but not enough to have me bent over in pain.

"What do you have balls of steel or something?" I heard the chick ask.

I turned around quick and snatched her up by her arm. I pulled her close cause I needed to make sure she heard exactly what I had to say.

"Bitch, if you ever do that shit again I'll have you leaking in a matter of seconds. Get ya shit the fuck together and get the fuck out of my club. We don't house rats here."

"Excuse you, but I'm not a rat. If you're that upset about me kicking you in the balls, then I can kiss them to make them better." She grinned.

"You wild as fuck ma, and I don't do those types. From how you lookin' you a walking STD, and I love a clean bill of health. Like I said tho you gotta get the fuck up outta here."

"I'm not going anywhere. This is my friends' party, and I'm here trying to have a good time."

"This my party and you ain't no friend of min..."

"Lola, why the hell you dart off like that? I told you to wait for us cause Paulie, and I had to use the bathroom right quick."

"Lola, what kind of kinky shit you into? You like getting' yoked up in the club?" the other chick with Promyse asked once they were closer to us.

Promyse gazed into my eyes, as I looked deep into hers. Surprise was written on her face, but I wasn't paying that any mind. Instead, my focus was on the tight red dress she was wearing. It was tight to the point it could've easily been mistaken for body paint. It hugged her every curve and suffocated her breasts. Her burgundy hair was in big curls that framed her face. Her legs were going on for days, and they looked silky smooth. My eyes trailed from her feet up back to her eyes. She was shittin' on the majority of the bitches in the club with no makeup on. She went the natural route, and she did it justice.

"Uh, why are you two lookin' at each other like that? You know him, Promyse?" Lola asked, looking between us.

"No, no, I don't know him. I was just trying to figure out why he had you yoked up?" Her words came out smoother than I thought they would've. She was lying, and that wasn't something I fucked with.

"I yoked her up cause shawty's mouth reckless, and I don't like that shit. Tell ya girl keep her feet to herself if she wanna keep 'em." I let Lola go then walked off towards the bar.

I needed a drink to calm me down cause I was seconds away from snatching Promyse up and bringing her ass into the bathroom. She had my head fucked up and my dick on brick. I wanted shawty something serious.

Chapter Twenty-Five

PROMYSE

"Who was that, Promyse?" Lola asked.

"I told you already that I don't know him." I pushed passed her and Paulie and headed to the VIP section. Everyone was in there including Bliss and Jiya. Smoke was turning up with a bottle in hand and a blunt in his mouth. I didn't want to ruin his fun, so I took a seat off in the corner.

What the hell is Saigon doing here? I asked myself.

Seeing him have Lola yoked up didn't bother me. What bothered me was the way he was looking at me. He was staring at me like he wanted to taste every inch of me and devour my middle. The look made me uncomfortable but turned on at the same time. I felt bad for feeling the way I was, but anytime Saigon popped up, I got the same feeling. It was intense and mysterious. A small part of me wanted to explore the feeling because it was alluring and Saigon was more than attractive. He was godly. The rest of me wanted to be with Smoke because he was exactly what I needed right now. I wasn't going to explore twenty percent of something when I already had eighty percent.

"Shit, if you don't know him I wouldn't mind getting to know him. He looks exactly like Method Man but finer. He just might be my future baby daddy."

"Lola, shut up with all of that." Paulie laughed.

"Laugh all you want, but I'm serious."

Lola and Paulie went back and forth about Saigon as I sat there trying to figure out what he was doing out here. Deep down something was telling me I shouldn't have been surprised that he was here. I decided to block all thoughts of Saigon from my mind because this night was about my baby. Tonight was a celebration for Smoke, and I wasn't going to spend it thinking about my fine ass stalker. I grabbed a bottle from off the table and raised it in the air.

"Hol up y'all my girl got something to say," Smoke said once he saw me with my hand raised.

All the commotion calmed down, and I could speak. I stood on the table to make sure my words were heard above the music.

"I just want to say congrats to my baby for making power moves. I'm proud of you and everything you've accomplished so far. This is only the beginning, and it's nothing but up from here. The Throne is your birthright, but it's already in your blood. Your father may have passed you the crown, but you were already a king in my eyes. You best believe your queen is going stand by your side, guard your heart, and protect your pockets. We a team baby and ain't nothing moving unless we say so. To Smoke and the rest of The Throne let's make street history." Everyone in the section cheered and took a drink.

Smoke came over and grabbed me in his arms. "That's my fucking baby!" he yelled kissing me sloppily. I kissed him back then wiped his lips so they wouldn't be glossy.

"I meant what I said Smoke; I got you."

"I know you did. Now let's turn the fuck up cause when we get home I'ma turn your ass the fuck out." He kissed me again then went back over to his boys. I laughed and admired my man.

"Let me find out my friend about to be a trap queen," Paulie said, snatching the bottle from me.

"I'm not saying I'm going to be all of that, but I am going to be anything Smoke needs me to be."

"I hear that. Now let's party cause who knows the next time we gon' be able to drink." She giggled.

Paulie, Lola, and I went in drinking and dancing the night away. By the time two in the morning hit, I was gone. My words were slurred, and I could barely walk.

I was so gone that I was two seconds away from peeing on myself.

"I have to go to the bathroom cause I'm about to pee on myself," I told Paulie.

"I'll come with you cause I don't need you falling into the wrong arms and Smoke having to fuck someone up," she told me.

"Where's Lola?" I asked.

"She left about an hour ago to go on the dance floor. She spotted someone she wanted to fuck with."

"And you just let her go? We're drunk we don't need to be alone," I told her.

"The only one drunk is you." Paulie laughed.

"I guess." I giggled. "Where's Smoke so I can tell him I'll be back?"

"I don't know. I'll text Khy and find out where they at while you're in the bathroom."

"Okay."

Paulie helped me up then guided me out of the section. The walk to the bathroom felt like it was taking forever. When we finally got to the bathroom, there was a line of five. I bypassed all of them and ran into the stall that a chick was coming out of.

"I know this bitch didn't just cut the line?"

"Yes the fuck she did, and her ass can get fucked up behind it once I pee."

A couple more chicks had something to say, and I paid their ass no mind. I finished peeing, washed my hands then walked out the bathroom the same way I walked in— untouched. Paulie was supposed to be waiting for me outside, but she was nowhere to be found. I walked around a little but didn't see her. The DJ was playing "Slow Motion" by Trey Songz, and my hips started moving. I somehow ended up on the dance floor. I started off dancing alone, but that wasn't how I ended the song. In the middle of the song, I felt someone grab my hips. They didn't grab them from behind like most dudes would've.

The bold individual grabbed them from the front, and when I looked the dude in the eye, I blushed slightly.

"Why blushing for?" Saigon asked.

"No reason," I told him and kept dancing. If I were in my right mind, I would've pulled away from him, but his hands on me felt so right in this moment.

"Turn around," he whispered in my ear.

I did as I was told and spun around, my ass grinded in slow motion up against him. He wasn't dancing with me or anything he was just standing there holding onto my hips firmly.

"Are you going to dance with me or just stand there?" I asked.

"I don't dance. I do other things."

"Oh yeah." I giggled but wasn't nothing funny, and he wasn't joking either.

The skintight red dress I had on started to move up as his hands slid up my thigh. He wasn't moving fast he was taking his time. His hands were dancing to the music until he got to my middle. He grazed my lips then softly kissed my lips. I took a deep breath and let it go.

"Let me touch so I can taste." His breath felt cool against my ear.

My body shivered against his touch. He took that as a yes then invaded my middle. His hands danced to the music as they went inside of me. They didn't stay there for long only long enough to get my juices flowing. He slowly pulled them out, spun me around, and placed his fingers against my lips coated them with my juices.

"What are you doing?" I questioned.

He silenced me with a forcefully kiss then licked and sucked my juices off my lip. I tasted myself when I slowly sucked his tongue. I knew I was wrong for doing what I was doing, but I couldn't stop myself. Saigon had complete control of my body.

"When you ready to finish what we started let me know."

"Huh?" I dumbly asked when he pulled away.

"You heard what I said. When you ready to finish this, let me know. Just make sure ole boy is out ya life. I don't play second," he told me then disappeared.

I stood there with a flushed face and wet panties. I somehow got myself together, and when I turned to walk away, Paulie was standing there looking at me and shaking her head. I grabbed her arm and headed outside so we could talk.

"Promyse, what the hell was that back there?" she asked when we got outside.

"How long were you standing there?"

"Long enough to know that wasn't Smoke touching and feeling in places that should only be touched by Smoke."

"I don't know what came over me. He just came up to me, I was drunk, and the music took over. Paulie I didn't mean to let that go down."

"And you said you didn't know his fine ass." She laughed.

"Why are you laughing? This isn't funny," I told her.

"Yes, the hell it is. You're so gone that come tomorrow you're not even going to remember this."

"True." I laughed too.

We continued laughing, but it was for two different reasons. Paulie was laughing cause she thought I had my first drunken moment that would make a good story later on. I was laughing because I wasn't drunk. The minute his finger grazed my lips I sobered up. I was fully aware of everything that was going on. It was like I said though I didn't have control of my body he did. My mind was screaming for him to stop, but my body wanted him to go.

"We gotta get back inside. I came looking for you because Smoke was looking for you."

"Okay, let's go."

I was happy as hell that it was Paulie who found me and not Lola. I know we started things over, but I still had my guard up. The trust between us wasn't there, and I didn't know what she would've done if she caught me. I knew Paulie good enough to know she wasn't going to say anything. That's why she was my girl through and through.

"Promyse, come here baby and let me introduce you to someone!" Smoke yelled from the back of the section.

I couldn't see him or who he was with I just heard his voice. I headed towards the back section, and when I got there, I damn near shitted on myself. Standing next to him was my stalker, the fine ass man I just let taste me— Saigon. I was confused on why he was standing next to Smoke. There was no way in hell that they knew each other.

"Come here, baby. I've been waiting all night to introduce you to my man here. It's about time he got here too. How you throw a party and show up late and shit?" he asked Saigon.

"I had business to take care of." He was talking to Smoke, but his focus was on me.

Fuck, what if Smoke can smell my pussy on his breath? That's not something that can happen, right? Promyse, stop being dumb. Ain't no way Smoke can smell your pussy on his breath.

"Business could've waited. We got bitches and bottles," Smoke said takin' a swing from the bottle he held in his hand. "Hol' up I ain't' mean to disrespect my girl like that. These niggas got bitches and bottles. I got bottles and my queen." He leaned over and kissed me on my cheek. An awkward laugh escaped my mouth.

"Baby, this is my boy Saigon. Saigon, this is my queen Promyse."

"Ma ya man's drunk cause he got that introduction fucked up. I'm not his boy. I'm his boss. It's nice to meet you.

"You too," I told him, refusing to look up at him.

"Smoke let me teach ya somethin' right quick." Saigon reached out and cupped my chin then slowly lifted my head up. "Never bow your head when you're introducing yourself. That shows weakness and a woman of your stature is anything but weak," he told me.

I held my breath as I waited for Smoke to go off on Saigon.

"You gotta do better by ya girl," Saigon told Smoke.

"Man, she's straight ain't nothing weak about my queen. You can believe that. I got this," Smoke gritted, pulling me closer to him.

"Chill out, man." Saigon smirked with his hands raised. "You ain't gotta pull her close cause if I wanted to pull her I could pull her. I'm just tryin' to school you on some shit. Don't take it personal."

"Ain't shit personal. Everything's love and business."

"Exactly. Straight business," Saigon said then walked away.

"That nigga actin' like he knows fuckin' everything. It's only a matter of time before I make them moves and take his crown. There's only room for one fuckin' king," Smoke gritted then finished off his bottle.

I should've hyped my man up and let him know that it was all about him, but I couldn't do it. My mind was too focused on how I fucked up so royally. I not only semi-cheated on Smoke, but I semi-cheated on him with his boss.

Chapter Twenty-Six

BLISS

"I'm ready to go this party's lame as fuck," I told Jiya.

Her ass was having the time of her life, but I was over it. The club wasn't my type of scene anyone. The only reason I came out was to show support to Khy and Smoke. Smoke told me about the party when he called himself checkin' me about what happened with his girl. Everything he said to me went in one ear and out the other. Anything he said that concerned his bitch wasn't respected cause it didn't come from her mouth. I hated when street dudes got these naïve chicks then wanted to fight their battles for them. What made this worse was him wanting Promyse to run shit. If she couldn't run her mouth and hold shit down for herself, there was no way she could hold shit down for him.

"I'm not trying to be a bad cousin or nothing like that, but I'm not ready to go."

"Then you stay, and I'll go back to the hotel."

"How are you going to leave me when I rode with you?"

"Have one of these niggas you ciphin' with bring you home or take a cab, but I'm up."

"You get on my nerves," she huffed but didn't stop blowing on her blunt.

"Yeah, I love you too," I told her and got up.

I wasn't about to play with Jiya. She already knew I didn't have a problem leaving her ass right where she was. This wasn't the first time I left her, and this wouldn't be last. Some might think I was fucked up for leaving Jiya, but I knew she would be straight. We both had our locations on and made sure that we shared them with each other at all times. If anything happened, it would be nothing for me to find her. Not that she needed finding cause Jiya could handle herself; she wasn't nothing to play and didn't take shit from a nigga or a bitch.

It took me forever to make it outside, but once I did, I headed straight for my car. A couple of the dudes that were outside chilling tried hitting me with that lame ass bird call they did. I didn't understand why dudes thought that would get a chick's attention. The "ayo ma you thick as fuck, or beautiful smile" lines were lame as fuck, but these niggas still tried to use them. A couple of them called out that I was ugly cause I didn't want to answer them and I laughed. They said women were emotional creatures, but that was a lie. These niggas out here were worse than females when it came to emotions. That was the exact reason why I was single and had been single for the last five years. I didn't have time to wipe the tears of a dude or feed their ego. I was too concerned with the money and making sure my daughter had the perfect life. Blessing was my heart. Nothing came before her and wasn't shit popping after her.

Her father, Roux was the first and last man to have my heart. He hurt me something deep but blessed me with something greater than that hurt. He claimed he never wanted to hurt me but didn't mind fucking any bitch that gave him the opportunity. I didn't have time for that so when he told me he was moving out of state to try and make shit shake. I let him go. He wanted me to come with him, but I couldn't bring myself to endure any more pain caused by him. I found out I was pregnant three months after he left and didn't bother calling to let him know. Roux couldn't do right by me and love me the way I needed to be loved, so I doubted he would be able to love his daughter. He wasn't going to break her heart the same way he did mine. I would rather leave my daughter fatherless then to see her hurt.

"Um, what are you doing on my car?"

When I was walking up on my car, I thought I seen a dude sitting on it, but I wasn't sure. The closer I got the better I was able to make the individual out. I was used to dudes looking at my car and taking pics, but none of them were bold enough to sit on my baby.

"This ya shit?"

"I asked why were you sitting on my car, right. That implies that it's mine and ya ass don't need to be sitting on it."

"Where ya nigga at cause this ain't ya shit."

"This why I don't fuck with you niggas. Y'all sexist as fuck. Why can't this be my car?"

"You're too prissy to be ridin' round in a 69 boss 429 mustang."

"Prissy, huh?" I laughed, moving closer to him.

"You heard me, ma." He smirked.

"Ain't shit prissy about me. Don't let this dress fool you cause I ain't got a problem shooting you in ya balls and stopping ya whole legacy. From what I'm guessin' you ain't bigger than a four which means ya balls won't be hard to find."

I was going to laugh but never got the chance cause this nigga snatched me by my hair. I was caught off guard cause no matter how much shit I talked to a dude they never put their hands on me.

"Cut the slick shit cause I'm not one of these lame niggas. I take threats seriously, and I handle them accordingly. Give me ya keys!" he demanded.

"I'm not giving you shit!" I spat.

"I can either kill you for that foul shit you said and trust me if I kill you won't a muthafucker alive be able to find you, or you can give me ya keys since this ya whip."

I bit the inside of my mouth cause this nigga was tryin' me. If he were anyone else, I would've called his bluff. The way he was talkin' and the certainty in his words told me he was really about everything he was talking. I went into my bag and got my keys.

"Take the car key off the ring."

I did what he was said and held it out for him to take. He let my hair go pushed me then got in my car. He started the engine and listened to it roar for a minute before pulling down the window.

"If you weren't such a bitch we could've taken this ride together. I would've fucked ya shit up then kicked you out in the morning. Shit would've been love, but ya mouth is slick as fuck. Have a good night tho." He smirked then pulled off.

I stood there looking dumb as hell. I refused to walk back towards the club and have them same niggas that were trying to get at me laugh in my face. I pulled my phone out and called a cab to take me back to the hotel. I didn't know who dude was, but I swore on God when I ran back into him, I was taking his life the same way he took my baby.

$ $ $

"Who the fuck is knocking on my door early in the fuckin' morning?" I spat while getting out the bed.

I looked at my phone to check the time, and it was only six in the morning. I was pissed someone interrupted my sleep but halfway thought it was the dude who jacked my car last night. Opening the door it wasn't the dude from last night standing at my door; it was Promyse's dumb ass.

"Why are you knocking on my door early as hell? Shouldn't you have ya man's dick in ya mouth or something?" I was in a foul mood and didn't care what came out my mouth at this point.

"I had his dick in my mouth a couple of hours ago. Want me to blow so you can smell it?" she asked, pushing past me.

I rubbed my eyes cause this wasn't happening right now. I was disrespected last night by a dude who disrespected me first, and now I was being disrespected by fucking Mighty Mouse.

"Look, I didn't come here to fight with you. I came here to have a conversation with you. I'm not going to be doing the back and forth jab for jab shit. I'm going to talk, you're going to listen, and then respond."

"I'm tired as hell, and I'm not feeling the way you're coming up in here talking to me. We can try this conversation at a later time cause right now ain't it."

"No, we're going to have this conversation now. You might as well sit down cause I'm not going anywhere."

I was going to sit down not because she told me to, I was sitting down cause I was too tired to remain standing up. I sat on my bed crossed my legs and folded my arms over my chest.

"Talk," I told her.

"I don't know where you got the perception of me that I'm privileged but you're wrong. There isn't anything privileged about me. Not everything I have was given to me. The majority of the clothes I wear are stolen from Rainbow. Anything else that I have that I bought I got with my money from stripping. I had to hustle to get everything I have. It may not have been the same hustle that you got, but I hustled."

"Yeah okay, you hustled. Is that supposed to make me respect you or something?"

"Yes..."

"Stop because you hustling ain't gon' make me respect you. The crackhead from around the way hustles every day to get their rocks. You think I respect them for that shit? Hell no, I don't. I don't give a fuck what you had to do to get what the fuck you have because it don't mean nothing to me."

"Then why did you bring it up? Why did you make it seem like me being privileged is the reason why you don't fuck with me."

"I didn't make it seem like it was the reason. I was letting you know what was wrong with you. Okay, you hustled for ya shit but now that you got Smoke you ain't hustling for nothing. You're not working your way up the food chain; it's being handed to you. You may not have been privileged before, but you damn sure are now." I paused for a second because I didn't feel like she was hearing me, and I needed her to hear.

"Look, I don't respect you because you didn't give me anything to respect. You walked in that restaurant thinking everything was going to be peaches and cream. Ain 't shit peaches and cream in this business. Every day we wake up is a day that we could die. We could lose our life in the blink of an eye, that's what gets respect from me.

The people I respect are the muthafuckers that get up every day and hustle because they want better for themselves or their family. The muthafuckers that live in their truth are the ones that I respect. Being in the trap ain't ya truth, but you're trying to live because ya man is telling you to."

"You don't know shit," she sassed.

"I know more than you think and that's why you're getting emotional. You don't want this shit. You're doing it because Smoke wants you to. You have no backbone or spine. You're weak, and I don't respect a weak muthafucker."

"I'm not asking for your respect because at this point I don't give a fuck about it. What I'm asking you is to teach me how to be the person I'm trying to be. I don't know nothing about this life, but I owe it to Smoke to be about this life. It's not because of what he's done for me, but what he's done for my mother. He helped my mother get clean when we weren't even together. Out of the kindness of his heart, he sent my mother to rehab and fixed up our apartment so that I would have a place to stay. He did that without me asking, and I feel like I owe him. This is the only thing he's asked of me, and that's why I'm doing it. I'm doing it because he asked me for one thing but has done so much for me. You might not understand that, but I don't expect you too. All I'm askin' is..."

"I got you," I told her, taking a deep breath.

"Wait what?" she asked shocked.

"You heard me. I got you. I can't teach you how to be about this life because it needs to be in you. I can teach you everything in the world, but if you don't have the strength or courage within you, then it doesn't mean shit. What I'm going to do is take you under my wing. I'm gon' show you how things go, but everything else will be on you. You're gonna have to make people believe that this is you because I'm not going to be able to."

"Thank you so much!" She smiled, jumping up.

"Uh huh, now get out."

She got up and headed for the door. Before she walked out, I called out to her.

"Yeah," she answered back.

"I can tell you're a good girl. Don't lose that innocence. It makes you who you are."

She smirked at me looked at the floor then looked back up at me. "I was a good girl 'til I knew him."

Chapter Twenty-Seven

PROMYSE

TWO DAYS BEFORE GRADUATION

"You still ain't heard anything about your car?" I asked Bliss.

We were riding around trying to find something to do. Any other day we would've been at the trap making sure everything was legit, but today was our off day. I was graduating in a couple of days and the last thing I wanted to focus on that damn trap house. I knew it was going to be hard work, but I ain't think it was going to be as hard as it was. Bliss had been teaching me everything I needed to know, and I was just getting the hang of it. Ten months working there and I was just now getting comfortable running things. The only thing that made it worth it was the money. I was stacking more money than I imagined I would. Money was good, school was good, my mom was still clean, but my man and I wasn't as good as we should've been.

We weren't have cheating issues or nothing like that, but we definitely had issues. I thought us working together would bring us closer, but it did the opposite. I barely saw Smoke unless we were fucking, or we had a meeting with the team. He was treating me like I was just another player on the team making him money. I've tried talking to him about it, and every time I did, he popped up with a new gift to say sorry. I would've went crazy if I didn't have school to keep me busy and Bliss by my side telling me not to trip cause this is what happens when you date a dude in the street. I started working out in Harlem to prove to Smoke that I was there for him to let him know that he could count on me for whatever. I did it to pay him back for everything he's done for me. I was doing this for him, and instead of being appreciative and loving on me, the nigga was still out doing what he was doing from jump, which was being that arrogant, cocky ass king of The Throne.

"Nope. I still can't believe some nigga had the nerve to jack me for my car. I swear if I wasn't in another state I would've popped him right then and there. It's cool tho, cause watch when I find him. He's gon' be left leaking, and that's word to my daughter."

"If you want I can ask Smoke does he know the guy. I would just need you to describe him to me."

"How you gon' ask Smoke to do anything when he's never around."

"Damn, I ain't know it was like that."

"I'm just saying. I know I told you that him being MIA comes with being with a dude like him, but to be honest the way he's moving is shady as fuck."

"I already know he's moving shady, but what can I do? I chose to be with him and to live with all that he comes with. Being busy is one of those things that he comes with."

"I'm just saying if you don't want to deal with it anymore, I won't blame you."

"I'm not breaking up with Smoke, Bliss."

"I'm not telling you to. I'm just saying you don't have to be with him because of what he's done for you. You don't owe him shit."

"I know that. I'm cool with how things are, and if there ever comes a time where I want to walk away, I'll do just that."

"Okay," she said, shrugging her shoulders. "What time are we supposed to be getting Paulie?"

"She's doing something with Khy right now, but I told her we would swing through later tonight."

"Is Lola coming?" Bliss asked with a roll of her eyes.

"Yeah." I laughed.

Bliss went from respecting Lola for speaking her mind to not caring for her. Bliss and I started off not really talking about anything besides work. After a while, we both started to open up to each other. I told her all about Lola and the things she's done. Bliss kept it real and told me I was dumb for keeping her as a friend. I had to tell her if I was dumb for keeping Lola as a friend, I was dumb for making her a friend. Lola did more fucked up shit then Bliss, but the shit Bliss did humiliated me and made me feel less than. In my eyes that was only a step down for what Lola did.

"I can't stand that girl," she huffed.

"I'm not a fan of Jiya's either, but I tolerate her."

"You don't have a reason not to like Jiya. If Paulie could get over the bullshit that happened, then you should be able to do it too."

"I'm not a fan of hers. I never said I didn't like her. She's always on ten and never wants to be on one."

"That's just how she is. Some people are low key and others are high key. She's one of them that are high key at all times. She means good tho."

"Let you tell it." I laughed.

"Anyway... How you feeling about graduation and your graduation party?"

"I can't wait to be over with school. I thought this year was going to be my year, but I barely graduated."

"I tried to tell you handling things out in Harlem and going to school was going to be hard. You insisted on doing it so don't complain now."

"I'm just saying that shit wasn't easy."

"Nothing in life is easy. But, what matters is that you're graduating, and the turn up is going to be real. Smoke may not be around, but at least he's throwing you a party."

"True. I just hope he stays. I don't need another repeat of my birthday." I sighed.

"Stop with all that sighing shit cause we don't need to be depressed right now. You're graduating soon and you're caking. You have so much to celebrate and the celebration starts now."

Bliss speed off down the street causing my hair to blow in the wind. I ain't know where we were going, but I was down for a celebration. We were supposed to be going out tonight and having a girl's night, but I was all for starting the turn up early. We ended up parked outside of a liquor store. We got out and all eyes were on us. Niggas were licking and biting their lips and the bitches were rolling their eyes and turning up their lips. It was crazy how once I became Smoke's girl I started to get evil stares from just about every chick I encountered.

"Ma, let me get a minute of your time!" one dude called out.

"Nah, I'm good," Bliss said.

"I wasn't talkin' to you shawty. Mind ya business. I was talkin' to ya friend."

"I'm good too. I don't do broke," I told him.

"Bitch, ain't shit broke bout me. I get money," he boasted.

I laughed at him and pulled out my phone. "That's right give ya boy ya number so he can upgrade ya shit. Have you out here livin' lavish, have you out in Paris."

I laughed to myself cause he didn't understand what was about to happen. I went through my playlist and found a song that was fitting for this moment. I wasn't about to go off on this nigga, I was gon' let my bitch Nicki do it for me.

"Have me out in Paris, huh? That shit sounds good, but let me play this song for you right quick so you can understand where I'm comin' from, big baller." I smiled.

I fast forward the song a little before pressing play...

Look at y'all sharin' one bottle in the club, one bottle full of bub ass niggas. Look at y'all not havin' game ass niggas, y'all niggas share a chain ass niggas. Same cup in the hand ass nigga. In the club with a credit card scam ass nigga. No dick in the pants ass nigga. I be damned if I fuck a non man ass nigga. I will never fuck a non man ass nigga. I would never lie, even if that nigga flew me and my bitches all the way out to Dubai.

I stopped playing the song because from the look on dude's face I got my point across. "So the moral of the story is I can't fuck with a nigga who says he moves ki's, but he really move grams, and he split it with his mans."

"BITCH!" Bliss yelled, laughing loud as fuck.

The dude's face was turning red, and I could see that he was upset. I was waiting for him to try something cause I was ready.

"Bitch, shut the fuck up and suck my dick!" he gritted.

I laughed because I knew this was coming. I hated when a dude got salty for getting played out. I was about to let his lame ass have it when the dude I've been avoiding for the last ten months walked up on dude.

"Watch what the fuck you say when you talkin' to mine. If you want ya shit played with I got a couple of bitches that wouldn't mind choppin' that shit up."

"Ayo, my bad, man. I ain't know this was you," the dude said sounded scared.

"Now you know so don't make the same mistake."

The dude didn't say shit. He just walked away in a hurry. I looked at Saigon and had to admit he was looking good. A little too good. After what happened at the club, I vowed to never let him get too close to me again. I was doing good up until this point. He walked right up on me and grabbed me in his arms. He kissed me softly on the lips like I was his girl and me kissing another nigga in public wasn't an issue.

"Uh, someone want to explain to me what's going on before I start lightin' niggas up," Bliss said.

"Wassup, I'm her future." Saigon smirked.

"No, you are not." I pushed him away from me and created some much-needed space between us. "This is my stalker."

"Stalker? Nigga, you are too cute to be stalkin' anyone." Bliss said.

"Tell me bout it. Ayo, let me talk to you right quick," Saigon said to me.

He asked to talk to me, but I didn't have an option. He grabbed my arm and pulled me off to the side.

"Why haven't I seen you lately?"

"I have a boyfriend, and he wouldn't be too happy with me if I were running around with his boss."

"You hear that shit that just came out ya mouth. Ya boy wouldn't be happy if he found you runnin' around with his boss. You're a boss fuckin' with the help. What kind of shit is that?"

"I'm not fuckin' with the help. I'm fuckin' with a nigga that I love. All this that you're doing needs to stop. I love Smoke, and I'm not going to do anything to fuck that up."

"Word?" he asked lookin' at me sideways.

"Word."

"I'm not hearin' that bullshit. Cut shit off with him. I'm ready to finish what we started in the club."

"I'm not cuttin' nothing off with nobody."

"I gave you ten months to get ya shit together. You ain't got no more time."

"You have to be crazy or something. Why are you talkin' like we're together or something? I don't know you, and you don't know me."

"Fuck that gotta do with anythin'? I'm telling you to cut shit off with ya boy and you talkin' bout knowing each other. The only thing I wanna know is that pussy. I told you I don't play second. Cut that shit off so I can have what I want, ight?"

"You're crazy as hell," I told him then walked away.

I headed towards where I left Bliss, but she wasn't there. I went to call her but stopped when I heard her loud ass yelling. I followed her voice and found her trying to swing on some dude that was tall and fine as hell.

"Bliss, what the hell are you doing?" I asked her, rushing over.

"Girl we bout to jump this muthafucker and then I'ma kill his dumb ass. This the nigga that stole my baby," she told me.

"It's been months, ma. This ain't ya car no more, it's my shit."

"Nigga, the only thing that belongs to you is the bullets in this chamber." Without a second thought, Bliss pulled her gun out in broad day.

"Bliss, put that away before the cops roll up or someone calls them," I told her.

"Stop trippin', ma. She ain't' bout to shot nobody. Her heart pumps Kool-Aid." Dude laughed.

"Fame, the fuck you got going on over here?" Saigon asked, grabbing me from behind.

"Will you get off of me please," I told him, trying to remove his hands.

"Chill the fuck out," he told me. "Fame, wassup?"

"Ain't shit. This is shawty I got the car from."

"This the chick that threatened to shot ya balls." Saigon laughed.

"Yeah I'm that bitch, and I'm glad y'all find this shit funny. Give me back my shit, and I might just spare ya life."

"Chill out shawty; we don't want that heat. Fame, give her back her shit."

"Fuck outta here! She was outta line talkin' that shit to a nigga she ain't know."

"Nigga, you were out of line for takin' her shit. Just give the shit back."

"Fuck you and this bitch!" the dude said and tossed the keys to Bliss. "Don't think ya ass is off the hook. Every time I run into ya ass I'ma cause you hell for that foul shit you said," Fame told her.

"Yeah what the fuck ever, nigga. Every time I see ya ass I'ma shoot you. Promyse let's go before I end up in jail fuckin' with this dumb ass."

"Can you let me go now? I have somewhere to be."

"Do what I told you, Promyse. Next time I see you I don't want no shit." Saigon let me go, and I walked away paying what he said no mind.

When we got in the liquor store, Bliss grabbed my arms and demanded I explain what the hell was that back there. I told her all about Saigon and what happened at the club.

"Bitch, I ain't know ya ass was creeping."

"I'm not creeping. It happened that one time, and I don't even know how it got that far. I don't know anything about him, but every time he comes around, I get all choked up and lovesick."

"I see why. That nigga is fine as fuck. His friend is cute too, but he got a fucked up attitude."

"Please keep this between us, Bliss. I don't need Smoke finding out about this cause it's nothing serious."

"You should know better than to tell me not to say anything. I don't get into people's relationship. All I'ma say is you better get it under control cause Mr. Saigon doesn't seem to be takin' leave me alone for an answer. He wants everything you have to give and then some."

"Too bad he can't get it," I told her.

Bliss didn't say anything after that. She grabbed the liquor she wanted, paid for it, and then we were gone. I followed her to her house in her car so that she could park it. I didn't know what I was going to do about Saigon, but something needed to be done. He was getting a little possessive and even though I liked how he handled me today nothing was going to come from it. He was a fantasy that I didn't plan to indulge in. Smoke was my one and only future and no one could change that. Not even Saigon's fine ass

Chapter Twenty-Eight

PAULIE

"You ight, ma?" Khy asked me.

We were walking through the mall trying to find me something to wear to my graduation. At a time, I should've been happy I wasn't. Things with Khy and I were great, but my mother and I still weren't talking. I tried to reach out a couple of times just to make sure she was doing okay. Every time I called, my mother she would answer then ask me was I still with Khy. Once I told her that I was, she would hang up the phone. After the fifth time of her doing that, I stopped calling. I wasn't going to keep calling for her to just hang up on me like I didn't mean anything.

She was being dramatic as hell, and she had no reason to be. She was trying to paint Khy in the image of my father, but the two were nothing alike. I didn't know my father, but I knew that Khy would never do what he did. Khy would never leave me alone nor do me dirty. I had faith in my man, and no one was going to change that.

What hurts the most about us falling out was the fact she didn't believe that she raised me right. She didn't have faith in me that if things did go left, I would leave with my head held high. Instead, she thought I would be like her. I would chase a nigga that didn't want to be caught until the end of time. She should've known better cause I wasn't in the business of chasing a damn thing.

"Paulie!" Khy said stopping me from walking. "You sure ya good? I've been talking to you for the longest and you ain't saying nothing."

"I'm fine. I'm just thinking about my mother. I graduate in a couple of days, and I don't know if she's going to be there or not."

"Don't trip off that cause ya moms is gonna be there."

"How you know?"

"Cause she's ya moms. No matter how mad she is with you, she's not going to miss an important day like ya graduation."

"She won't even talk to me tho."

"Ya moms means well she just doesn't know how to deal with you being a mini her. No mother wants their child to follow in their footsteps to heartbreak. When she looks at me, all she sees is ya pops. It's not right, but I get it. She just wants the best for you."

"Yeah well, little does she know you're what's best for me."

"Say that shit again," Khy said, grabbing me in his arms.

"Nah, I don't need you getting a big head and shit." I laughed.

"I already know I'm that nigga." He laughed too.

"Aw ain't this cute. Khyree, who's this?" Our laughter ended, and the smile on my face disappeared quickly. Some big booty bitch was standing in front of us looking between Khy and me.

"Sweetie, you don't have to stare at me like that cause I don't mean no disrespect. Khyree and I are old friends. We grew up together his grandma used to babysit me. If anything Khyree is like a little brother to me. Khyree, tell her." The chick smiled.

"Baby, this is Mercy. Mercy, this is my wife Paulie."

"Oh, you got married! Congratulations!"

"Uh, we're not married but thank you. Come on Khy we have to go."

I grabbed Khy's hand and pulled him away.

"Khyree, who was that bitch?" I asked

"A chick from back in the day. My grandma used to watch her," he answered without skipping a beat.

"You sure because she looks real familiar."

"They say everyone got a twin." He laughed.

I laughed slightly, but nothing was funny. I couldn't put my finger on it, but I swore I've seen that girl before. I've never questioned was Khy faithful before and I wasn't going to start now. I trusted him, and until he gave me a reason not to, I would believe what he said.

$ $ $

"But baby don't get it twisted. You were just another nigga on the hit list. Tryna fix your inner issues with a bad bitch. Didn't they tell you that I was savage. Fuck your white horse and carriage. Bet you never could imagine. Never told you, you could have it. You needed me..."

The DJ was playing Rihanna's song "Needed Me". For some reason, I was vibing to the song more than usually. It had me in the mood to fuck a nigga's head up just because.

"Rihanna knew what she was doing when she made this song. This that national fuck a nigga song," Jiya said, dancing and sipping on her drink.

"You ain't never lied. On God when this song comes I be feeling like the baddest bitch in the room. Have me in the mood to tell a nigga you got it twisted we ain't on that lovey dovey shit," Lola added in.

"You okay, Paulie?" Promyse asked me.

We were the only ones in our section not drinking. Since Jiya and Bliss were twenty-two they were able to buy their drinks. Lola had a fake ID, so she was straight. Promyse and I were only eighteen and didn't know anything about getting a fake ID. Instead of having Bliss buy our drinks, we just chilled out. I didn't know about Promyse, but I was still vibing from our pregame session.

"I'm fine. I just have a lot on my mind." For some reason, the chick from the mall was still in my thoughts. Something about her seemed so familiar, and my brain wasn't going to rest until I figured it out.

"We can talk about it if you want."

"I'm not about to have a Dr. Phil moment in the club. I'm good, Promyse."

"Okay, but we're going to talk about this later on." I nodded my head at her then got up and started dancing.

We're supposed to be celebrating, and I wasn't going to let some random bitch stop me from having fun. The rest of the night was pretty much a blur after my talk with Promyse. Turn up wouldn't even be the right words to describe our night. We turned that club the fuck out and left with no regrets. When the club let out, we headed to where Bliss and Promyse had parked.

"I needed a night like this," Lola said.

"Why? What you have going on?" Jiya asked her.

"Nothing much, just issues with my mom. The way she be movin' stresses me out. Then I thought me and my dude was rockin' heavy, but he's been duckin' me lately. I ain't heard from him since the night we went to that party out in Jersey."

"Bitch, if a nigga went missing for ten months that means he's no longer ya nigga. Let that shit go and find you a new one or get some double A batteries." Bliss joked.

"Batteries wouldn't do me justice. All I can think about is tasting his chocolate stick and bitter milky filling."

"Ew Lola," Promyse said screwing up her face.

"Don't act like you don't suck the dick," Lola told her.

"Yeah, I suck the dick, but I'm not running around telling everyone about it."

"Y'all ain't everyone." Lola shrugged then laughed. We all laughed with her cause she was stupid ass hell.

"Ight let's go I'm ready to get home," I told them.

I was about to get in the car when I heard someone calling my name from a distance. It was a female voice, so I stopped to see who it was. I didn't rock with females other than the ones I was out with tonight. So, for a female to call my name, she must've had something important to say.

"Paulie! I'm so glad I caught you," Mercy said when she got closer to me.

"Paulie, do you know this bitch? She looks thirsty," Lola said, eying Mercy.

"The only thing that looks thirsty is ya hoe ass!" Mercy spat.

"Takes one to know one, trick," Lola sassed.

"Chill out with the bullshit, Lola. I have on my red bottoms and don't need to be fuckin' these up cause you got us in a fight," Jiya told her.

"Mercy what do you want? If you're looking for Khy, he's not with me."

"I wasn't looking for Khy I was actually looking for you. I wanted to come to you as a woman and tell you—"

"Did this bitch just say she's coming to you as a woman?" Bliss asked, cutting Mercy off.

"Paulie, say the word, and I'll handle her," Promyse told me.

"Promyse it's cool cause I don't need you to handle anything. This bitch ain't coming to me as shit cause she ain't got shit to tell. I know my man, and he wouldn't ever fuck with a low-class bitch as ya self."

"That's where ya wrong hunny because he..."

"Bitch, you a little hard of hearing!" I yelled after I punched her in the mouth. "Like I said my man would never fuck with a low-class bitch like ya self. We don't do thirsty over this way boo. Let's go," I told the girls.

Instead of getting in the car with Lola and Promyse, I got in with Bliss and Jiya. I already knew Promyse and Lola were going to have a hundred and one questions that I wasn't ready to answer. I didn't realize where I knew Mercy from until she hit me with that coming to you as a woman bullshit. That was the bitch from the hotel. After the party, out in Jersey Khy and I went back to our hotel room to get it popping. I got the room first cause Khy and Smoke were talkin' about something and Khy wanted me to go upstairs to get ready for him. When I got in the room, Mercy was in there starting to get undressed. I ain't go off or nothing like that cause when she saw me, she jumped then asked me what the hell I was doing in there.

I explained to her that this was my room and she was in the wrong. She checked her key card and realized she was in the wrong room. She laughed saying that was why her key card didn't work. She left out the room before Khy could get up upstairs. I thought she made an honest mistake, but after tonight I realized I was the one who made the mistake. Either Khy fucked that bitch, or he was on the verge of fucking her.

I didn't know which one it was, but for right now I was going to let it be for the moment. My graduation was coming up, and I didn't want anything messing up my day. But best believe when my graduation was said and done with Khy was going to have hell to pay and the devil to answer to.

Chapter Twenty-Nine

KHYREE

"You deadass buying Promyse a condo?" I asked Smoke.

Smoke hit me right when I was about to lay down and catch some Z's. He told me he had something to show me and to come by his crib. Paulie was out with her girls, so I headed out. I was trying to catch up on some much-needed rest. Shit had been moving crazy lately and sleep became foreign. I thought we were moving weight before, but that shit was small time to what we were doing now. The money was coming in hand over fist and to make sure there were no fuck ups, we were working around the clock.

"Yeah, my nigga. Promyse deserves this shit. She stepped up in a big way. She's handling shit out in Harlem and graduating. Most chicks would've folded with the hectic schedule Promyse had, but my girl's too strong for that shit she's handling it like a champ, and this is her reward." I nodded my head cause the place was dope. It was four bedroom, two-bath condo out in Queens.

"Plus, I don't need shawty out the Ps anymore. Her name is buzzing in the streets because of the work she's putting in. Most know she's my girl, but that ain't gon' stop a nigga from trying her. The last thing I need right now is someone running up in her spot and pulling the trigger."

"Nigga, say God forbid or something. Don't speak that shit into existence."

"I'm fucking untouchable and so is my bitch. I'm not speaking nothing in existence. I'm just saying in case a nigga does try to run up I'm not tryin' to make it easy for him. Not too many people are going to know about this place here. Promyse is gon' be good."

"Keep talkin' that untouchable shit. Ain't no one in this world untouchable," I told him.

Smoke had this way of thinking that no one could get at him. I tried to talk to him about that bullshit before, but he wasn't trying to hear it. He swore he was the baddest muthafucker around. I knew better. When it came to niggas at the top, no matter how many goons or guns you had around if someone wanted to touch you bad enough, you would get got.

"You talkin' like you got something in the works or some shit," he said with a raised eyebrow.

"I don't even get down like that, and you know it. It's nothing but love between the two of us. I'm just saying chill with that untouchable shit. You ain't doing shit but making niggas wanna touch ya just to say they did it."

"I ain't worried bout no lame trying to come up off my downfall."

"I feel you. But yo if you tryin' to keep Promyse safe, why not let her come stay with you?"

"I need my space. You and Paulie be arguing like y'all ain't got no sense. I'm not trying to go through that shit. I like to be alone sometimes and only wanna be bothered when I want to be bothered. Don't get me wrong I love having Promyse around, and that's my heart, but a nigga still wants to do him without having her all up in my business."

"You cheatin', nigga?"

"Nah, I'm not creeping. I'm just saying if I wanted to the option would be open for that shit cause I live dolo. Then I'm not trying to have her mom all up in my shit. I like ma dukes, but she be lookin' at me sideways and shit. I don't need that smoke." He laughed,

"She probably be pissed about y'all fucking in her crib and shit."

"She needs to get over that shit if that's what she's trippin' over. When I need to bust a nut, I handle my business. I don't give a fuck where we at. We could be at her mom's crib, at the supermarket, or in the club. I'ma handle my business when the time comes."

"Nigga, you a whole fool." I laughed.

"I'm talkin' straight facts tho. On the real, I'm just not ready to let Promyse in my space. We doing good, and I want to keep it that way without adding any more bullshit to it."

"I feel you."

If I had a choice on whether Paulie and I would be living together, that shit would be a no. It's not that I didn't like living with Paulie, but the shit was forced onto me. I went from giving her a key for when she would spend the night to living with her all in the blink of an eye. Everything was cool right now, but it took a lot to get to the point where we were. We argued like crazy and fucked like lunatics. Our relationship was bipolar on some real shit, but we some how managed to make it work.

"I'm thinkin' bout giving her the keys the night of her graduation party."

"I can see that," I told him.

Smoke kept talking, but my attention wasn't on what he was talkin'. While he was going on about the party, a couple of text messages came through to my phone. The first couple of messages were pictures of Paulie out at the club. The next text that came through told me who was texting me and had me ready to fuck some shit up.

929-434-6328: I know I said I would play second, but I changed my mind. I wanna be ur one and only. Meet me at this address, or I'll tell your girl all about our fuck sessions. Yeah, nigga plural.

Right after that, a message with an address came through. My jaw flexed as I sent a text back to Mercy.

Me: Do what u gotta do ma. I ain't trippin' off that shit.

That stunt Mercy pulled early was some bullshit, but her ass wasn't bold enough to step to my girl with the bullshit.

929-434-6328: Oh so you're trying to call my bluff. That's cute.

Me: Like I said do you, ma

929-434-6328: Fine, don't say I didn't give u the opportunity to stop this.

"Nigga, you ight? Ya big ass over here turnin' red and shit."

"I'm straight. I'ma catch you later. I got something to handle."

"Ight."

I dapped Smoke up real quick then left out and jumped in my car. I thought about going to the address Mercy sent, but I wasn't bout to be her bitch. I thought Mercy was gon' be able to keep shit on the low. I ended up fuckin' one more time after the first time. I couldn't even tell you why I did that shit. She came onto me, slipped, and my dick caught her by the mouth. Once I felt the back of her throat, it was love from that point on. She wasn't letting me go, and I didn't want to go. I felt bad for fucking up again, but a nigga was only twenty-one. I was young and was gon' make mistakes. Not saying that was a valid reason, but the shit was the truth. I pulled off heading to my house. Mercy knew who the fuck I was and what I was capable of. Killing wasn't something I played with lightly. I only killed when the shit was necessary. Mercy stepping to Paulie bout the bullshit would have her signing her own death certificate.

$ $ $

"Wassup ma, how as the club?" I asked Paulie when she walked in our bedroom. The dress she had on put all the bullshit I had on my mind to rest. The only thing I wanted to do was have Paulie climbing the walls.

"It was cool," she said. Her response was dry as fuck.

"Why you sound like that? Who I gotta fuck up?" I asked her. Mercy never sent another text. I figured her ass came to her senses and left the club. From the way Paulie was acting tho, I knew something had to happen.

"Nothing just tired. Lola was actin' a damn fool, and we almost go into a fight with these chicks."

"You betta not be fighting behind that bitch. I already told you to leave her hoe ass alone."

After that bullshit she tried to pull on me about having HIV, I went and got checked. My shit came back clear, and I made sure to make it clear to Paulie that I ain't want her fuckin' with Lola. Shit didn't go in my favor cause I couldn't give her a real reason why I didn't want her fuckin' with Lola. I damn sure wasn't gon' tell her she sucked me off, so I bit the bullet for the time being.

"That's my friend, Khy. The same way she would fight for me is the same way I'm going to fight for her. What you do tonight?" she asked with an eyebrow raised.

"Nothing, I been chilling in the house. Why wassup?"

"Nothing, just asking."

"Paulina come at me with what you gotta say. All this beating around the bush shit ain't you. Say what you mean and mean what you say," I told her.

"The girls and I were having a conversation about dudes in the game and the woman who hang on to them. Bliss and Jiya were saying that every dude in the streets cheats at least once."

"Don't listen to that bullshit. Bliss and Jiya are some bitter bitches that ain't never fucked with a real nigga. They're speaking from experience of fucking with a fuck boy. You got a real one on ya team. You ain't got shit to worry about."

"That's what I told them. What we got is real and ain't no way you would cheat on all of this." She smiled running her hands over her body.

She was out of her dress and only in her bra and thong. I licked my lips ready to run my tongue all over her body.

"You're licking your lips like you wanna taste something."

"I mean if you got something for a nigga to taste then bring it here." I told her.

She came over to the bed and crawled to the middle. She laid on her back then wiggled out of her thong. She shot it up into the air, and I caught it with my mouth. I looked at her in amazement as her skin glistened under the light in the room.

"Are you going to stare at me or give me what I've been missing?" she purred.

"Get up and sit on my face," I demanded.

"You sure you can handle all of that. I wouldn't want to drown you."

"A nigga knows how to hold his breath." I smirked.

"That's my type of dude." She smiled then climbed on my face.

She slowly rocked her hips back and forth against my tongue. I moved it in a snake-like motion tasting her before she knew she was leaking. Her pace went from slow and steady to fast and wild. She was rocking and popping her hips. Her grinds weren't subtle if I were some weak nigga, I would've been all fucked with the way she was moving.

"Ahhhhh!" she cooed out loud. I grabbed her ass and stuck a finger in her ass. She stiffened up at first then got comfortable.

"Yesss Khy! Just like that! Just like that, daddy!"

Her moans were exotic and had me on brick. She wasn't cumming fast enough for me. Once she got hers off, I was trying to bend her ass over, and that shit moves like a wave in the ocean. I flipped her over and dived in without warning. I made circular motions around her clit with the tip of my tongue then started writing the alphabet. My tongue was the pencil, and her clit was my paper. Her back arched and her nipples got hard.

"Fuck!" she whispered when I started taking long licks of her clit all the way down.

"How do I taste?" she asked in between moans.

"Sweet, ma." I shoved my tongue into her opening

snaking it up and down. She gripped my head, pulling me deeper as she exploded on my tongue.

She was breathing hard as fuck. I continued licking up and down until I got her to the point of no return.

"Khy...Khy...Khyreeeeee!" she shouted.

Hearing her scream my name was music to my ears. Her body went into convulsions as I slurped up her juices.

"Bend that ass over," I told her smacking her thigh.

"I'm tired and need to shower," she said, rolling off the bed.

"You can shower after I'm done," I told her. "I'm tryin' to fuck you silly."

"I'ma have to take a rain check cause I really just want to shower and go to sleep."

She kissed my cheek, wiped the corner of my mouth, and then left out the room. I sat at the edge of the bed trying to figure out what the fuck just happened. As if she knew my dick was on hard, my phone started blowing up and Mercy was the caller. A nigga was tempted to answer it and get my dick wet, but I couldn't keep doing that bullshit to Paulie. On the other hand, she did leave a nigga with a hard dick and a wet tongue.

Chapter Thirty

PROMYSE

"Today is our graduation day, and you're really killing the vibe, Paulie." Lola said.

We were all at my house getting ready to head over to the school. Paulie was sulking looking like she lost her best friend when she should've been smiling and laughing with Lola and me. I didn't know what was going on with my girl, but ever since the other night when that bitch stepped to her on that fake woman shit, her mood had been off. I tried talking to her about it, but she would just change the subject. I figured when she was ready to talk about it she would.

"If I'm killing the vibe then move the fuck around!" she spat.

"Woah relax! It's not that deep," Lola told her, rolling her eyes.

"Yeah, whatever," Paulie said.

"This is not what we're about to be doing. Today is our day, and we're not going to ruin it by arguing about bullshit. Paulie, you need to check ya attitude cause today is supposed to be a happy day. Lola, stop being a bitch cause now isn't the time."

"I'm not being a bitch. I'm just telling Susie sad ass that she needs to fix her attitude. No one wants to be around her while she's like this."

"No one asked you to be around me. You can get the hell on, Lola."

"Let me leave before I say some disrespectful shit. Promyse, I'll meet you at the school. Hopefully, Ms. Bitch will be in a better mood."

"Fuck you, Lola!" Paulie shouted.

"I don't swing that way boo." Lola laughed while she was walking out the house.

"Paulie you really need to change ya attitude."

"My attitude won't be changing no time soon."

"What's wrong? Paulie, talk to me cause I'm not letting you got through this day with an attitude."

"It's just that—"

"Wait hold on, this is Smoke calling me." I didn't mean to cut her off, but I've been blowing up Smoke's phone since I woke up and his ass wasn't next to me.

"Smoke the only words that need to be coming out of ya mouth right now is that your outside and ready to go," I told him skipping the hellos.

"Yo watch the way you talkin.'"

"I'm not going to watch anything. Where did you run off to this morning that was so important?"

"I had business to handle."

"Why am I not surprised!" I spat.

"What's that supposed to mean?"

"It means that whenever it comes to something important, you have business to handle."

"Man you're exaggerating. Stop being dramatic."

"Oh, I'm not exaggerating. Do you remember what happened on my birthday?" He got real quiet on me, but I wasn't about to let him off the hook. "Don't get quiet on me now. If you don't remember, I don't mind filling you in. You set up a huge scavenger hunt for me. I got the last clue and met you at the Sugar Factory all for your ass to show up two fucking hours later."

"I told you some shit came up."

"No, you told me some shit came up and you would be half an hour late after I was already waiting for thirty minutes. Smoke I'm not playing with you. You need to be outside in the next five minutes."

"I'm not goin' be outside in the next five minutes so let's cut all that bullshit out."

"Then what are you calling me for?"

"I'll meet you at the school. Drive over with ya mom."

"Really! Smoke Really!"

"Chill out cause the shit isn't that deep. I got caught up and what I'm handling is taking longer than expected. Just head over there, and I'll be there to watch you cross that stage."

"Don't even bother coming!" I yelled, feeling frustrated.

"Promyse lower ya tone cause you gettin' mad when shit ain't that deep. Just head over there, and I'll meet you there. I love you."

Smoke didn't give me the chance to say I love you back or anything. The nigga hung up leaving me to reply to the dial tone. I threw my phone on the dresser and let out a frustrated scream.

"Mhm let me guess he has business to handle?" Paulie said.

"How you know?" I asked her.

"Cause it seems that the nigga always has business to handle. Any time it comes to something important he has business to handle. Hell, you barely see his ass unless he wants sex or calls a staff meeting. You need to make sure that nigga ain't cheating."

"Wait why would you say that? You think Smoke is cheating?" I questioned.

Paulie never really said much when I would vent to her about Smoke and his lack of presence. She would tell me pretty much the same thing Bliss would. That he was a street dude and him having limited time came with the territory.

"All these niggas do is cheat. He's a street nigga one at the top of the food chain at that. He got bitches by the dozen that want to get at him. You think he's not out there smashing something? If you think that shit, ya stupid."

"I'm not stupid, and Smoke isn't out there smashing nothing. He's busy because he's at the top of the food chain." I said defending my man.

"Yeah okay, that's what I thought. I thought I had a good man one that loved me and would never do me wrong. I was dumb as hell. I should've listened to my mother because she knew better. She told me Khy would fuck me over and that's exactly what he did."

"What you mean Khy fucked you over? I know you're not believing what that bitch said at the club." What Paulie said about Smoke didn't matter anymore. She finally opened up about what was bothering her, and what I had going on Smoke wasn't important at the moment.

"Promyse, I believe everything she said. Why would a random bitch lie about fuckin' my man when she doesn't know me nor does she owe me anything."

"Paulie she's lying just to get your spot," I told her.

"I don't even want to talk about this right now because it doesn't matter. My dumb ass got played. Khy played me good." She laughed.

"Paulie, you're not dumb."

"Yes I am Promyse, and it's okay. Cause I'm done with that nigga and any other nigga that thinks about coming my way. Now come on so we can go and get this graduation over with."

My heart was hurting for Paulie because she was taking this hard, but there was no way that Khy cheated on Paulie. They were relationship goals in my eyes. They acted like best friends but loved hard like lovers.

"What if Khy did cheat on Paulie? That would mean Smoke cheated on me cause they're always together. Smoke ain't gonna sit there and watch his boy get his dick sucked and not partake in the activities," I said out loud.

As fast as that thought came I put it to rest. Smoke wasn't cheating on me, and Khy wasn't cheating on Paulie. Smoke was extremely busy because he was running The Throne. That was what he told me, so that was what I was going with. I didn't have time to deal with this anyway. It was my graduation, and after that, I would be turning up at Club Lust. It was my day, and I was going to enjoy it.

$ $ $

The turnout for the graduation party had me feeling myself even more. Smoke and Khy rented out Club Lust, and it was a good thing they did because the turnout was a lot bigger than I expected. Everyone from school came out to show love. People from around the way came out, and of course, the crew came out for us tonight. It was overwhelming because I wasn't used to getting this much attention. For the first time in my life, I was feeling real important. All night people were stopping me telling me congratulations and how proud of me they were. I never thought having strangers telling me they were proud of me would put a smile on my face, but it did. I couldn't even lie I was starting to feel like I was THAT BITCH.

Not only was I feeling like that bitch, but I was looking like that bitch. Smoke went out of his way to get me a custom-made black silk sleeveless wrap dress. It hugged my body like a newborn baby and left very little to the imagination. On my feet were simple black shoes that had my legs looking like they went on for days. Smoke didn't stop at the custom-made dress, he got me chandelier diamond earrings, a necklace, and a bracelet to match. My burgundy hair was bone straight with a part in the middle. My makeup was simple, but still gave me a glow that had every dude in the place turning heads.

Smoke went all out for me, but it was to be expected. It wasn't expected because he wanted me to look good on my night, it was expected because yet again he fucked up and was trying to make up for it. Not only did he not ride with me to my graduation, but his dumb ass didn't make it to my school in time to see me walk across the stage.

I was beyond hurt because during the ceremony I kept looking towards the back to see if he would walk in. With each name that was called Smoke was still nowhere to be found. When my name was called he still wasn't there. He had the nerve to walk in as soon as I stepped off the stage. I couldn't bring myself to argue with him because my feelings were beyond hurt. Instead of letting him win and fuck up my night, I took the L and acted like nothing was wrong. I was tired of arguing with him when he always failed to realize where he fell short.

"Both of you are about to get cut off. Y'all are too lit," Lola said to Paulie and I.

When Paulie and I got back to my house, we made a promise to each other to enjoy our night. We were both going through issues and because of that we decided to drink our pain away. Paulie was way more drunk than I was, but I wasn't too far behind her.

"Girl, let us live. We just graduated high school," Paulie said, dancing in her seat.

"Y'all can live all y'all want just chill out on them drinks," Lola told us.

Paulie and I both looked at each other then busted out laughing.

"Come on, girl. Let's go thank these people for coming out. Grandma Lola is blowing mine," Paulie said, pulling my arm.

"Bitch, don't disrespect me like that." Lola laughed.

"Then don't disrespect us by telling us to chill out," I told her.

"Fine do what y'all want, but I'm not holdin' back anyone's hair."

"Hush and just come on." I grabbed her wrist, and the three of us headed towards the stage.

I signaled for the DJ to stop playing the music then picked up the mic.

"Uh, excuse me. Could I have everyone's attention for a minute."

Everyone stopped what they were doing and looked our way. It was a good thing I had one too many drinks in me because if this were any other time, my ass would've been sweating bullets. Instead, I was confident and smiling like a damn Cheshire cat

"I would just like to thank everyone for coming and celebrating with us tonight. There isn't anyone I would rather share this moment with than my two best friends who are standing beside me. Lola and Paulie, the both of you have helped me through so many troubling times in life that it makes no sense. We fought and bickered, but we always found our way back to each other. I couldn't ask for better best friends. Today we walked across the stage and put high school behind us. We are embarking on a new journey in our lives, but no matter what I will always be here for the two of you. Instead of allowing life to trouble us, let's make a promise to give life trouble." I smiled. I gave my girls a quick hug then went back to talking.

"I can't forget to thank the man that came into my life and changed it for the better. Smoke baby, I wouldn't be who I am without you being in my life. I was a good girl until I met you, and I never want to go back. There isn't nothing I wouldn't do for you in this world. I would kill for you and even get ya name tatted on my pussy for you." I giggled as everyone else in the crowd gasped.

"What I'm trying to say is I'ma always be your ride or die chick. No questions asked I'm blastin' on any nigga or bitch that tries to stop us from being one. I love you, baby. Come up here and give me a kiss."

I was all smiles as I waited for Smoke to come up on the stage and kiss me.

"I don't think he's coming," Lola whispered to me.

"Shut the fuck up bitch cause he's coming!" I spat.

As the seconds went passed, I started looking out into the crowd to see if I could find him. It took me a minute to find him, but when I did, I caught him running towards the exit along with Khy.

"OH HELL NO!" I yelled, dropping the mic and running off stage.

I heard Lola and Paulie calling me, but I ignored them and rushed outside. The cool air hit me like a ton of bricks when I got outside. I paused for a second to find where Smoke ran off too. I spotted him and called out to him before he could jump in his car. I kicked off my shoes and ran towards him as fast as I could.

"Smoke! Smoke!" I yelled.

"Promyse, take ya ass back inside ma. I'll be back go enjoy ya night," He told me.

"No Smoke I'm not going nowhere until you tell me why you keep running off." I kept quiet when he missed me walking across the stage, but I wasn't going to keep quiet now. This was my night, and he should've been by my side.

"Promyse, I need you to go inside and wait for me to come back. I'll be back right after I go handle this...."

"Business!" I spat finishing his sentence. "I'm so tired of you saying that you have business to handle. There isn't that much fuckin' business in the world for you to handle. You had business to handle on my birthday,

Valentine's day, while I walked across the stage, and now at my damn party. How many times are you going to use that as an excuse? If your fucking someone else just tell me. I'm a big girl. I can handle it."

"Get the fuck out my face with that bullshit. When I tell you I'm handling business that's what the fuck I'm doing. Ain't nobody out here fuckin' bitches."

"Nigga, stop fuckin' lying. If that nigga is out there fucking bitches then so are you. You ain't just gon' watch him get his dick sucked without getting yours sucked too," I slurred.

"Hol' up you outta line Promyse. I ain't out here fuckin' no one," Khy told me.

"Nigga, please! Ya lies don't work on me. Ya bitch came to Paulie like a woman and told her the bullshit. Let her ass know tho I'ma come to her like a woman and cap a buss in her ass!" I spat. I wasn't sure if that was how the saying went, but I didn't care at this moment. I was pissed off and talking my shit.

"Promyse, you outta here wildin'. Go the fuck back inside, and I'll get up with you later."

"Shaheem, I'm letting you know now. If you get in that car and fuckin' drive off, then I'm going to fuck someone else tonight!"

I should've known better than to say that shit but I had all the courage in the world thanks to the liquor. Smoke didn't say anything right away. Instead he yanked me towards him by my arm. This nigga yanked me so hard I felt my arm pop and thought he popped it out of place.

"Promyse, play with me if you want to and that's ya fuckin' life." His words were simple and straight to the point, but they were ice cold. "Now get the fuck back inside and don't leave here until I get the fuck back." He let me go and shoved me.

I fell to the ground on the side of the car crying my eyes out cause it was true, Smoke was out here fuckin' someone else that meant way more to him than I did. Call me crazy, but he didn't even threaten me like he gave a fuck if I fucked someone else or not. Yeah, he threatened my life, but there was no real emotion behind it. He just sounded cold and cold wasn't enough for me.

That liquid courage I had a minute ago was gone, and the tears started to fall. "Fuck you, Smoke!" I yelled as he got in his car.

"I better be the only nigga you fuckin'" He gritted. Smoke had the nerve to roll the window back up and pull off.

I stayed on the ground as people looked at me crying. I was tired of Smoke and his bullshit. Him never being around was one thing, but him never being around when it counted had me ready to throw in the towel. I thought I could be the kind of woman Smoke needed by his side. I thought I could be that down ass bitch, but it was clear he had someone else playing that role. It should've dawned on me a long time ago that I was the side chick, but my ass was too caught up. I was too caught up to see I was getting played.

I started to get up off the ground but felt a pair of arms pull me up. "Thank you, but I didn't need you to help me I'm good!" I snapped, dusting myself off.

"Ma, you need my help. That nigga got you out here on the ground cryin' and shit when tonight's ya night. You shouldn't even be going through this bullshit right now."

His voice stopped any tears that were falling from my eyes. The sadness I felt disappeared when I turned around to look in his eyes.

"You're saying all of that like you wouldn't have done the same thing. All you street niggas are the same."

"Ain't shit the same about me. Don't group me in the same category as that lame ass nigga. That nigga's a thug; I'm a boss. He can't compare where the fuck he doesn't compete."

"Mhm, let you tell it."

"Fuck letting me tell it, let me show you."

He cupped my chin then stopped any response I had with a kiss that was as deep as the ocean. I didn't hold back kissing him like I've done in the past. I feel deeper into the kiss the more he nibbled on my lips.

"You cuttin' that nigga off, right?" Saigon asked me, ending our kiss.

"Fuck that nigga," I told him with a smile. I didn't really know what I was doing, but it felt like the right move.

Smoke wanted to be out here fuckin' bitches, so I was going to give him a taste of his own medicine. It was only right an eye for an eye was how I was going to play it.

$ $ $

Saigon was looking at me with lust-covered eyes. I was laying on the hotel bed ass naked waiting for him to take my pain away. He brought his lips to mine, and that's when my river started to flow. His lips devoured mine, and the feeling of his soft lips against mines sparked something in me that I never knew existed. I shoved my tongue into his mouth, craving his taste. This feeling that I was going through was new to me. Smoke made me feel good every time we kissed, but he never made me feel like this. The sensation Saigon was giving me just by placing his lips against mines was intense.

His tongue went from exploring my mouth, to my neck, and then to my earlobe. It wasn't long until his wet tongue glided against my nipples. They became milk duds upon contact. He kept licking, sucking, and nibbling on them until I moaned his name.

"Saigon," I cooed, loving the feeling his tongue was giving me.

He roughly spread my legs, cupped my butt in his hands and lifted my hips so that his mouth was only an inch away from what was going to be his late night snack. The way he worked his tongue sent chills up my spine. Gentle flicks of his tongue brought me close to my peak, but every time he would get me there he pulled away. He released my butt from his grasp allowing my body to drop back against the bed. Lowering his body back on top of mine, he was staring at me with the same lustful gaze as before.

I gazed back at him with the same intensity. For a quick second guilt washed over me. I loved Smoke with all of me and sleeping with Saigon wasn't going to change or take away the love I had for him.

"AHH!" I screamed out as he bit the side of my neck.

"Don't second guess this shit cause I'm what you need. I'm the nigga you've been waiting for. I'm that nigga that's going to better you mind, body and soul. Ya old nigga was simply that a lesson. Baby, I'm ya blessing," he told me.

He bit me again and entered me at the same time. I wanted to gasp for air, but there was no air for me to gasp. He held himself in place, and I swore I felt my insides expand. Not letting go of my neck, Saigon began to long stroke me. I had no choice but to endure the slight pain his dick was giving me. He had length and width, which was something my pussy wasn't used too.

"What do you want?" Saigon questioned, letting go of my neck.

"I don't know!" I moaned out. The slight pain I was feeling before subsided after a while. I was feeling nothing but pleasure as my hips bucked.

"What do you want?" Saigon asked again.

"I don't know."

"Wrong fuckin' answer. The next time you say that bullshit I'ma leave you with a wet pussy," he gritted.

He was having a full-blown conversation but never missing a beat when it came to his strokes. I was starting to get dizzy from the pleasure he was bringing me. Him stopping was out of the question.

"What do you want, ma?"

"I want you!" I moaned out.

"You want me, or you want this dick?"

"I want youuuuuu!" I cooed out in pleasure.

"Ight then." He kissed me on the lips, then pulled out.

"Wait, what are you doing?" I questioned in a panic.

"You said you want me, so you don't get this dick." He smirked.

"I want both," I pleaded. "Finish giving me what I want Saigon, please," I begged.

He got back on the bed, roughly grabbed my legs, and then put them on his shoulders. He slipped back in and the air I wasn't able to gasp before was not there. He pumped roughly in and out of me, but I didn't care because the pleasure was intensified.

"Fuck, this pussy is good," Saigon groaned. He gripped my thigh and I thrust my hips forward. I was giving him all I had to offer because he was giving me everything I needed.

"Whose dick is this?" He asked throwing me off guard.

"It's mine!" I cried without thinking twice.

"That's the shit I like to here. Give me that gushy!" he demanded.

My body must've understood what he was saying because I exploded all over his dick. I was screaming out in pleasure and looking into this eyes. The way he was biting his lip led me to believe he wanted to scream out just as loud as I did.

"Promyse, you're mine now. That lame left you scarred now a real nigga bout to reinvent you," he groaned as he reached his peak. I felt his seeds slipping into me as my walls tightened around him.

"Been waiting on that sunshine boy, I think I need that back. Can't do it like that. No one else gonna get it like that. So I argue, you yell, but you take me back. Who cares when it feels like crack? Boy, you know that you always do it right. Man, fuck your pride. Just take on back, boy take it back boy. Mmm, do what you gotta do, keep me up all night. Hurting vibe, man, and it hurts inside when I look you in your eye."

"That's ya phone?" Saigon questioned looking at me.

"Yeah, I need to get that," I told him, trying to move from under him.

"Nah that can wait. I'm tryin' to go another round."

"We can do that, but that might be one of my friends. I ran out of the club and didn't tell them where I was going."

"Where ya phone at?" He asked.

"It's in my purse," I told him waiting for him to get up so I could get it.

"Ight, hol' up."

Saigon got off of me and grabbed my purse. I sat up in bed thinking he was going to hand me my phone so I could answer it, but he did the opposite.

"Yo." He said answering my phone.

"What are you doing?" I whispered jumping off the bed.

"Hello? Promyse? Is this Promyse?" I heard Lola say.

I snatched my phone away from him and took it off speaker. I rushed to the bathroom then closed and locked the door behind me.

"Yeah, Lola what happened?" I asked.

"Promyse, where are you? You gotta come quick! Smo...Smo...Smo...Smoke got shot up!" she yelled frantically.

To Be Continued

STAY IN TOUCH
With Kellz Kimberly

Facebook: Kellz Kimberly

Instagram: Kellzkimberlyxo

Twitter: xoKellzkxo

Snapchat: Kellzkayy

Facebook Reading Group: I Read, I Sip, I Slay

OTHER BOOKS

By Kellz Kimberly

The Deception of Love 1-3

Trinity 1-2

Ain't Nothing Like a Brooklyn Bitch 1-3

Jealous 1-2

Falling For A Real Nigga 1-4

All She Wanted Was A Rider 1-3

Down For My Nigga 1-2

A Player's Prayer (Standalone)

Gunz & Laci (Standalone)

He Got Me In My Feelings 1-2

Lay My Heart On The Line For You 1-2

She Gotta Be The Dopest To Ride With The Coldest 1-2

Love & The Come Up 1-3

A Thug's Blessing 1-3

Every Bad Boy Needs A Rider 1-2

She's My Lil Hood Thang (Standalone)

CPSIA information can be obtained
at www.ICGtesting.com
Printed in the USA
LVOW03s2324190118
563260LV00001B/199/P